THE VANISHING DEATH

Thieves, breaking into a mortuary to steal the body of a woman, are disturbed by a police constable, and they escape, dropping their burden in the street. Then, days later, a lorry grazes a speeding car, dislodging a hamper attached to its roof. Neither vehicle stops. Inside the hamper, the police find the body of a recently murdered man whose corpse had been stolen whilst awaiting police examination. Who's behind the would-be body-snatcher — and what is their sinister purpose . . . ?

NIGEL VANE

THE VANISHING DEATH

Complete and Unabridged

LINFORD
Leicester

First published in Great Britain

First Linford Edition
published 2011

British Library CIP Data

Vane, Nigel.
   The vanishing death. - -
(Linford mystery library)
1. Body snatching- -Fiction.
2. Detective and mystery stories.
3. Large type books.
I. Title II. Series
823.9'12–dc22

ISBN 978–1–4448–0746–2

Published by
F. A. Thorpe (Publishing)
Anstey, Leicestershire

Set by Words & Graphics Ltd.
Anstey, Leicestershire
Printed and bound in Great Britain by
T. J. International Ltd., Padstow, Cornwall

This book is printed on acid-free paper

1

The Mystery of the Hospital

The fine weather and the need of fresh air after a day at his desk, had induced Philip Quest to go for a long walk that evening at the close of the summer.

He had tramped as far as Hampstead Heath, and was on his way home between ten and eleven o'clock, strolling leisurely down Southampton Row, when, for no particular reason, his mind reverted to a curious affair which had occurred a week or so before.

The mortuary attached to the hospital in the Whitechapel district, had been broken into one night and the body of a woman had been stolen. The sudden appearance of a constable, however, had frightened the thieves as they were carrying the corpse through a dark passage to the street. They had dropped their burden, taken to flight, and escaped in a motor car that was waiting in the vicinity. The constable had been unable to give any description of them, beyond stating that they were two well-dressed men, and no light had yet been thrown on the mystery.

That the body had been stolen for dissection was the only theory which could be entertained, but it was not a very plausible one. Yet there could have been no deeper motive, it seemed, since the woman was the wife of a poor labouring man.

It was rather odd, in view of what was so shortly to happen, that Quest should have recalled the affair at this time. He had no more than ceased to think of it when he heard shouts in front of him, and saw a closed car approaching at a high speed.

As it shot by he had an indistinct glimpse of the man who was driving. He shouted himself, but no attention was paid to him.

He turned to gaze after the car, which swerved sharply to the right, then hastened forward to where a number of people were standing in the middle of the road.

They were gathered round a large hamper, of the size used by actors on tour, and amongst them was Inspector Deering of the local police, whom Quest knew well. With some difficulty he pushed his way into the crowd and reached the Inspector's side.

'What's all this about?' he inquired.

Inspector Deering shrugged his shoulders.

'Nothing of much importance,' he answered. 'There was a slight collision here, just as I was passing, between a lorry and a car. The two grazed each other and this hamper, which was on the top of the car, was thrown off into the road. It dashed on and so did the lorry.'

'I noticed the car,' said Quest. 'It flashed by me and swung into Circus Road.'

'Did you see the number of it?'

'No. I didn't. It was going too fast and was showing no rear light. And I only had a vague glimpse of the man who was driving. I wonder what's in the hamper, Deering?'

'I don't know. It's padlocked. I daresay it contains laundry linen.'

'No, it's much too heavy to hold linen,' declared Quest, as he lifted an end of it.

The Inspector did the same.

'You're right,' he assented. 'Do you think we ought to open it?'

'I certainly do. This seems to me to be very suspicious. The occupants of the car were in a great hurry to get away. They didn't stop or even slacken speed, though they must have heard the shouts.'

'Yes, it does look suspicious, Mr. Quest. We had better investigate.'

The padlock was a small one and it was not securely fastened. Inspector Deering wrenched it off, using the blade of his knife and raised the lid of the hamper.

It was a gruesome sight that was revealed. Within the big hamper, lying there in a huddled position, was the body of a man — a man of middle age, decently dressed, with a scrubby black moustache and a crooked scar on his cheek.

'Good Heavens! No wonder the car didn't stop!' gasped the inspector. 'This looks like a murder!'

'It does,' agreed Quest.

'There can't be any doubt about it. What a pity you didn't see the number of the car! Did you notice what colour it was?'

'Dark blue, I think. I can't be quite sure.'

Quest closely scrutinised the corpse.

'No, we're wrong,' he said a few seconds later. 'It is not a case of murder.'

'I don't see that it can be anything else under the circumstances,' Inspector Deering replied.

'I can,' answered Philip Quest in an odd voice. 'It's a case very similar, I imagine, to the strange affair in the Samaritan Hospital, Whitechapel, a couple of weeks ago. You know about that, I suppose?'

'Yes, I remember that clearly.'

'Well, an early edition of the evening paper today stated that the body of a man had been found floating in the Thames this morning and taken to the Rising Sun public house at Wapping. The paper said there was no clue to the man's identity, and it gave a full description of him. Did you read it?'

'Not carefully, Mr. Quest. I saw the paragraph but merely glanced at it.'

'Then you will be interested in the description of the man. He was stated to be a man of middle age, fairly well dressed, with a small black moustache, and a crooked scar on his left cheek.'

The Inspector gave a quick start.

'That seems to fit the description of this corpse!' he exclaimed.

'It does,' replied Quest.

'You think it is the same person? You believe this body was stolen from the public-house at Wapping?'

'There is every reason to believe it. And in all probability the thieves were the same men who attempted to steal a corpse from the mortuary of the Samaritan Hospital.'

'I'm inclined to agree with you, Mr. Quest. I feel there is some slight room for doubt, though.'

'Little or none!' declared Quest. 'It can

hardly be only a coincidence that the description of the man in the newspaper corresponds with that of the corpse in this hamper. But I can easily settle the question, I shall go to Wapping at once.'

'And I'll come with you,' said Inspector Deering. 'I'm not on duty tonight.'

During the conversation the exciting news had spread. Many more people had assembled, and they were proving troublesome when several constables came on the scene.

They handled the crowd, and Quest and Deering, after instructing the police to have the hamper taken to the police station, set off in a taxi.

'If my theories should turn out to be right,' Quest remarked as they started, 'I shall be strongly inclined to take up the case. I have felt from the first that there was something extraordinary about the hospital affair.'

'I thought so, too,' said Inspector Deering. 'I don't believe it was the work of medical students wanting a body for dissection, though Scotland Yard held that opinion.'

Quest nodded.

'I know they did,' he answered, 'and I told them that they might learn some day that they were wrong.'

They drove through the deserted city down the gloomy stretch of Nightingale Lane to the river, and thence by docks and wharves to the Wapping High Street, reaching their destination towards twelve o'clock.'

The Rising Sun was not closed, though it should have been at this hour. Lights shone within and the door to the bar was partly open. A constable was posted outside of it, and a few people were standing on the pavement on the opposite side of the road.

The constable recognised Philip Quest as he stepped from the cab with his companion, and touched his helmet to him.

'Have you heard the news already, sir?' he asked. What the question meant was unmistakable.

'So the body that was found in the river this morning has been stolen?' Quest replied.

'It was carried off tonight, sir,' the constable assented. 'Taken from the shed at the rear of the public house.'

'I thought so. A corpse of a similar description was found in the West End not more than an hour ago. It was in a hamper that was jolted off the top of a car in Southampton Row.'

'Ah, then the thieves had a car, Mr. Quest! I didn't know that. It was a neat piece of work and done very quietly.'

'Wasn't there anyone watching the body?'

'Yes, sir, one of my mates, Dick Burrows. He was attacked unawares and knocked on the head.'

'Was he badly hurt?'

'No, sir, he's pulling round now. They've got him inside.'

'Well, we'll go in,' said Quest. This is Inspector Deering of Southampton Row.'

He entered the Rising Sun with his companion and they went through the bar to a small room at the back. There were several people here; the landlord and his wife, the potman, a doctor, and a young constable, who was sitting limply in an armchair.

He was very pale and there was a dazed look in his eyes. He had so far recovered, however, that he could recall what had occurred and was able to talk lucidly.

Quest introduced himself and Inspector Deering to the landlord and the doctor, and when he had briefly explained what had brought him to Wapping he spoke to the constable.

'Tell me just what happened,' he said. 'I want all the information you can give me.'

'That won't be very much, sir,' Dick Burrows answered. 'But tell me, did they get the body?'

'Yes, it was stolen. And recovered afterwards in another part of London.'

'Recovered, was it? I'm glad of that. And the men sir?'

They escaped. They were in a car and the corpse, which was in a hamper, fell off the top of it into the street. Go on with your story now and tell me as clearly as you can. You were taken by surprise, I believe?'

'That's right, sir. The body was in the

shed at the bottom of the garden, and the men must have come through an alley to the garden wall, and climbed over it. They — they could easily have — '

The constable's voice faltered. He paused for a moment, pressing his hand to his forehead and complained of dizziness. The doctor gave him some brandy and water and he soon recovered.

'It was very stuffy in the shed, sir, with a lantern burning there,' he continued. 'I stepped outside for a breath of fresh air, and was walking along the path, in the direction of the house, when I was hit on the head from behind. I dropped like a log and the next thing I knew I was back in the shed, lying bound and gagged on the floor.'

'There were two men there, standing by the corpse, and talking in low tones. Both were tall and both wore black masks. I could see that one was clean shaven. His mask barely covered his nose, while the other had a long mask that came down to his chest.'

'They lifted the body and were about to carry it away when they noticed that I was conscious. One of them — it was the one with the long mask — poured something from a bottle on to a sponge and pressed it to my face. The drug put me out, and I remembered nothing more until I came to my senses in this room a little while ago. That's all, sir.'

The landlord turned to Quest.

'I discovered Burrows, sir,' he said. 'I went out to the shed with some sandwiches for him and a pint of beer and found him on the floor, unconscious. I called my potman and after we had carried the poor fellow into the house I sent for the doctor and the police.'

The narrative was unsatisfactory. The meagre information lacked anything in the nature of a clue. But the detective questioned in the hope of learning more than he had been told.

'Can't you give me a better description of the men?' he asked.

'I'm afraid not, sir,' replied Dick Burrows.

'How were they dressed?'

'The one with the short mask was shabby. His clothes looked cheap and common, and he had coarse, thick boots on. The other was very respectably dressed, and he wore patent leather shoes.'

'Were they dark or fair?'

'I couldn't see. Both of them wore caps.'

'Do you think the one with the long mask had a beard and moustache beneath it?'

'It struck me he had. I can't be sure.'

'Did you hear any of their conversation, Burrows?'

'No, sir, I didn't catch a distinct word. But the man with a short mask had a rough sort of voice as if he wasn't educated, and from what I could judge the other talked like a gentleman.'

'You believe he was an educated man?' asked Quest.

'I should certainly think so,' the constable answered.

'Did you notice his hands.'

'They were clean and smooth, sir, with long, thin fingers.'

'And the man with the short mask?'

'He had rather dirty hands, with thick, stumpy fingers.'

There was nothing further to be learned from Dick Burrows, and nothing from the landlord. Neither he nor his potman could give the slightest information.

Questioned by the detective, both declared that as a rule they served only regular customers, and that no strangers had been in the bar during the last couple of days.

Quest departed with Inspector Deering and stopped outside to speak to the constable at the door.

'Were enquiries made immediately after the discovery that the body had been stolen?' he said.

'Without delay, sir,' the constable replied. 'My chief inquired of various people in the neighbourhood as soon as he got here.'

'With no result?'

'None, Mr. Quest. Nobody had seen any suspicious characters in the vicinity of the Rising Sun.'

'The corpse was not identified in the course of today, I suppose?'

'No, sir, it was not.'

Quest and the Inspector were no wiser than they had been before. Their suspicions had been proved to have been correct, and that was all. They drove away in their taxi — they had kept it waiting — and Quest was in a silent mood, until they had got beyond the City.

'As there is not the faintest clue to work on, to give me a start,' he said at length. 'I'm afraid it would be useless for me to try to carry on with the case. There are several points which stand out clearly, however. It is to be presumed that the well-dressed man with the gentlemanly voice — he probably wore a long mask to conceal a beard and moustache — is a person of superior education and culture, and that the other, the shabby man with the rough voice and the stumpy fingers, is a person of very different type, very like an ordinary crook who was paid for his assistance. And there can be no reasonable doubt, it would appear, that these men are the same two who stole a corpse from the Samaritan Hospital.'

Inspector Deering nodded.

'There seems to be no doubt at all,' he

replied. 'As for the man with the long mask, perhaps he is some famous surgeon who has a private dissecting-room.'

'If so he could afford to purchase bodies. That's not a very plausible theory.'

'No, I admit it is a bit weak. Have you any other theory to offer?'

Quest shook his head.

'No,' he said. 'I am completely in the dark. I cannot conceive of any motive that would fit in with the circumstances of these two cases of body-snatching. But I'll tell you two things, Deering. In the first place, there will almost certainly be a third attempt to steal a body. And in the second place it is strongly in my mind that when the truth comes to light, if ever it does, there will be a sensation that will shock and horrify the public!'

2

Robert Ferris' Strange Story

After the affair at the Rising Sun, Philip Quest was engaged on important work for a time, but even had he not been busy he would not have taken the case of the two body-snatchers in hand, since, as he had told Inspector Deering, there was nothing to give him a starting point.

The meagre information furnished by Constable Burrows was of no value, and there was nothing in the way of a clue in the identification of the man found in the river, for it was discovered that he was a petty tradesman of Walham Green who had failed in business.

The interest of the public was not very deeply stirred. The newspapers held to the opinion that the perpetrators of the two crimes had wanted the bodies for dissection, and as for the police, they were inclined to agree with the Press.

More than a week had passed, and there had been no other mystery of the kind, when one morning Philip Quest received a letter from Robert Ferris, of Scotland Yard, asking him if he would kindly call there at his earliest convenience.

Robert Ferris was a modest man, and an uncommonly shrewd and clever one, of whom the public rarely heard. Though he was a member of the C.I.D. — he was virtually the Chief — his exploits in that capacity were seldom mentioned in the papers. He let others have the credit, partly because he did not care for notoriety and partly because, having many dangerous enemies, it was advisable that his movements should not be chronicled.

From time to time in past years the Government had employed his services in the Secret Intelligence Bureau, and had sent him abroad on missions of a difficult and perilous nature. He had travelled all over Europe and fluently spoke most languages.

He was an intimate friend of Philip

Quest's, who had the highest opinion of his capabilities.

Quest had more than once gone with him to some foreign country at the request of the Intelligence Bureau, and when he drove down to Scotland Yard that morning, after the receipt of the letter, he supposed that he was going to be asked again to assist in some secret task. He was to learn that he was wrong.

He was well known at Scotland Yard and on his arrival there went straight through to an inner room that overlooked the Embankment, and was very plainly furnished.

Robert Ferris was at his desk, which was littered with documents. He was a lean, loose-jointed man of forty, with clean shaven features.

'It was good of you to come so soon, Quest,' he said as he shook hands with him. 'I wished to see you rather urgently, and I am so busy that I couldn't get the time to call at your place, else I should have spared you this inconvenience.'

'It's no inconvenience,' Quest replied. 'I'm not very busy at present.'

'So much the better. I can count on your assistance then.'

'Is it to be another trip abroad, Ferris?'

'No, nothing of the sort. Quest, I'm worried. A friend of mine has disappeared and I want you to help me to find him, if he is alive.'

'If he is alive? You think he is dead then?'

'I have reason to fear so, Quest. That is why I wrote to you. All my men at the Yard have their hands full, and — '

Robert Ferris broke off.

'I will tell you the story briefly,' he said. 'I think you are acquainted with Pierre Renault, the French detective, who is head of one of the special brigades of the Sûreté, in Paris.'

'Yes, I have known him for some years,' answered Quest.

'Well, I had a letter from him a week or so ago,' said Robert Ferris, 'asking me to let him have what information I could gather about a certain Dr. Francis Burgin, of 6, Lime Grove, St. John's Wood. I made enquiries myself and learned nothing to the discredit of the gentleman. His 'dossier' was in every respect favourable. He has been living at the address in St. John's Wood for the last four years. He pays his bills promptly and bears a good reputation in the neighbourhood. He leads a somewhat secluded life.

'Very few people call at his house, but he has a small circle of friends of high standing. He is a Britisher — or is said to be. He speaks various languages, and is believed to have lived on the Continent before he settled in St. John's Wood. He has plenty of money, I gathered. He is not a physician, he's a scientist. His degree was conferred on him by the University of Prague for some scientific discovery.

'So much for that. To continue. I wrote to Pierre Renault, and had a reply from him saying he was not satisfied with my report, and was coming over to England shortly. It was at the end of last week I heard from him. Early on Monday evening, three days ago, he called at Scotland Yard while I was absent, and left a note for me. It was to the effect that he had just arrived in London and was staying at the Universal Hotel in Leicester

Square; that he was going to make enquiries himself, and would call at the Yard again on the following morning.

'He did not come. On Tuesday afternoon I went to the Universal and was told that Pierre Renault had gone out on the previous evening and had not since returned. No message had been received from him. His bag was in his room and I was allowed to search it. I found only clothes.

'My friend has been missing for three days, and I have not been able to get any news of him. He could not have met with an accident, I have enquired. He simply vanished into the maze of London, leaving no trace. And there the matter rests. What do you think of it?'

Quest was deeply interested.

'It certainly looks bad,' he said. 'You have no idea, I suppose, why Pierre Renault wanted information about Dr. Burgin?'

'None in the least,' Robert Ferris replied. 'He did not enlighten me on that point.'

'Why not get in touch with Lamant, the

Chief of the Paris Sûreté, he might know something.'

'I wrote to him yesterday, Quest, and I should have an answer tomorrow.'

'There was no mention of the disappearance in the papers.'

'I had it suppressed. I felt that it would be advisable.'

The detective nodded in agreement.

'I presume, from the note Renault left for you, that he went to St. John's Wood on Monday evening to make enquiries about Dr. Burgin.'

'There can scarcely be a doubt of it,' replied Ferris.

'And he may even have called at the doctor's house.'

'That is what I have been thinking.'

'You are afraid he has met with foul play, Ferris?'

'To be perfectly frank I am, Quest,' replied Ferris. 'I see no other reasonable explanation for his mysterious disappearance.'

Quest nodded gravely, and then:

'Have you seen Doctor Burgin.'

'Not yet,' answered the Scotland Yard

23

man. 'I have been waiting until I heard from the Chief of the Sûreté.'

'Why wait? I should like to have a look at the Doctor. Let's go there now and ask him a few questions.'

'It will put him on his guard if he is guilty.'

'I don't think it will do any harm. We can be careful not to alarm him.'

Robert Ferris hesitated for a moment.

'Very well,' he said. 'We'll go now. Perhaps I ought to have gone before. How much should we tell Dr. Burgin?'

'We will have to be discreet,' Quest replied. 'You had better leave the talking to me.'

They left immediately, picked up a taxi on the Embankment, and in less than half an hour were outside Number 6, Lime Grove, St. John's Wood.

It was a detached residence of three stories, standing back from the road in well-kept grounds, and surrounded by trees.

The door was opened by a servant, a clean shaven, square headed man, and having been informed by the visitors that they wished to see his master on private business, he ushered them into a luxuriously furnished library.

Shortly afterwards Dr. Francis Burgin appeared; a man of middle age and powerful build, nearly six feet in height, with a complexion that was the colour of old ivory, a jet black beard and moustache, thick dark hair, and piercing eyes that were as dark as his beard which flowed over his chest. It was obvious at a glance that he was no ordinary person. His domed forehead was intellectual, and he had a masterful, commanding presence.'

'Good morning, gentlemen,' he said in a quiet, well modulated voice. 'What can I do for you?'

He waited for an answer. Without a word Quest offered his card, and when Dr. Burgin had read the name that was engraved on it his face lit up with a genial smile.'

'My dear Mr. Quest,' he exclaimed, grasping his hand. 'I am delighted to make your acquaintance! I have read a great deal about you, of course, and your detective work had a special interest for me because you so often supplied scientific principles to your deductive theories.'

He paused again.

'If I may modestly say so,' he went on, 'I had somewhat of a reputation for scientific and analytical research when I led a more active life abroad than I do here in England. Perhaps you wish me to put my knowledge at your disposal in some way?'

The detective shook his head.

'My companion is connected with Scotland Yard,' he replied, 'and I have come with him to make some enquiries concerning a friend of his, a Frenchman of the name of Pierre Renault.'

The doctor's face showed only blank surprise.

'Renault?' he murmured. 'The name is not familiar to me. I have never heard of the gentleman.'

Philip Quest was regarding him closely.

'Pierre Renault,' he said, 'is the head of one of the special brigades of the Sûreté in Paris. A couple of weeks ago he wrote to Scotland Yard asking to be furnished with information about a certain person. That person was yourself, and — '

'He wanted information about me?' Burgin interrupted in a puzzled tone. 'Extraordinary!'

Quest nodded.

'The enquiries were made,' he continued, 'and Pierre Renault was informed by letter that you were a gentleman of irreproachable character. He did not let the matter rest at that, however. He arrived in London last Monday and took a room at the Universal Hotel in Leicester Square. He left the hotel early in the evening, presumably with the intention of coming to St. John's Wood, and he did not return. He has not been seen or heard of since. He has been missing for three days.'

'You suggest that he meant to call on me on the Monday evening, sir?'

'I thought he might have done so, Doctor. That is the reason for our visit.'

Dr. Burgin shrugged his shoulders.

'I am sorry I can't help you,' he said calmly. 'I know nothing of this Pierre

Renault. He has certainly not been to my house. And I repeat that I have never heard his name before. It is eight or nine years since I was last in Paris. I have never lived there and I have no friends or acquaintances there.'

'Thank you, Doctor,' said Quest. 'We do not doubt your word. It is to be feared that the French detective has fallen into the clutches of some of the dangerous crooks who infest London.'

'Or he may have been killed in a street accident, Mr. Quest.'

'Maybe. It is not likely, though.'

'I want you to be clearly convinced that I have no knowledge of the man, sir,' said the doctor. 'Will you search my house?'

'Oh, no. We should not dream of subjecting you to such an indignity!' Quest replied.

'As you please. I should not offer the least objection. But I am curious to know why Pierre Renault desired to have information about me. Can you tell me that?'

'No, doctor, I cannot. Neither of us has the least idea what his motive was. He did not give any explanation when he wrote to Scotland Yard.'

There was nothing more to be said. Quest and Robert Ferris took their departure, and walked along Lime Grove looking for a taxi.

'Well, what do you think?' enquired Robert Ferris.

'What is your opinion?' asked Quest.

'I'm baffled. I don't know what to think. The doctor was perfectly cool and self-possessed all the time. He appeared genuinely surprised. There was not the slightest sign of guilt or uneasiness.'

'Not the slightest, Ferris. I was watching him closely. The man has a most striking personality. What a pity we don't know why Renault wished enquiries to be made about him! Has the doctor a black past? Renault must have had some reason to suspect him. What else could account for — '

Philip Quest broke off.

'I firmly believe,' he continued, 'that Dr. Burgin knows something about the disappearance of your friend Renault.'

'I have been waiting for you to say

that,' replied Robert Ferris. 'I believe it myself.'

'Yes, your friend must have called on the doctor on Monday evening. And what happened?'

'Heaven only knows! We ought to go back and search the house.'

'Not now,' said the detective. 'Wait until tomorrow. You will have had a letter from Paris by then and it will probably throw a light on the mystery. Here's a taxi. You can drop me at my office.'

3

The Letter from Paris

Philip Quest called again at Scotland Yard the next morning at eleven o'clock, and as soon as he entered Robert Ferris' room he was handed a letter. It was from the Chief of the Sûreté, and it ran as follows:

'Dear Monsieur,
'I am distressed to learn of the strange disappearance of my colleague, Pierre Renault. I trust he will be found alive and well.

'I was surprised to hear that Renault had asked Scotland Yard to have enquiries made about a Dr. Francis Burgin, residing in London. I had no knowledge of that for I was not taken fully into his confidence. The name of Dr. Burgin recalls nothing to me, and I am unable to give you any information of a helpful nature.

'From what little Renault told me all I know is this.

'He had by chance overheard a conversation somewhere in Paris which led him to suspect that there was living in London a criminal whom the French police have been wanting to get hold of for some years. He did not mention the man's name and I did not enquire. I was very busy at the time. When I last saw Renault, on Sunday night, he said he was leaving for England in the morning, and that he expected to make a most sensational discovery.

'Please spare no effort to clear up this strange affair. I shall await further news with impatience.

'Yours faithfully,

'Henri Flamant.'

Quest read the letter with care and shrugged his shoulders.

'This is most unsatisfactory,' he remarked.

'Very,' said Robert Ferris. 'We are no wiser than we were before.'

'In a sense we're not,' Quest replied. 'This letter now allows us to draw some plausible deductions. Pierre Renault's suspicions were correct. The conversation he overheard related to Burgin. He is the man referred to by the chief of the Sûreté as the criminal wanted by the French police. I feel certain that Renault foolishly called on the doctor on Monday evening to verify his suspicions.'

'And walked into a trap,' said Robert Ferris. 'What do we do now?'

Philip Quest's lips tightened and his face was hard.

'Accept Dr. Burgin's offer and search his house and garden,' he said.

'And what if he refuses to let us?'

'Oh, no, he won't! He's too shrewd to make that blunder. He feels perfectly safe and for that reason I doubt if we will discover anything. We'll have a try, anyway.'

A few minutes later they left Scotland Yard, each with an automatic pistol in his pocket, and drove to Lime Grove.

The servant opened the door of Number 6, and Dr. Burgin, who was in the hall, saw the visitors and led them into the library.

'I suppose you have come to search, gentleman?' he said blandly.

'With our apologies,' assented Quest, 'and your permission.'

'Most certainly,' replied the doctor. 'I have nothing to conceal.'

'You have no objection, Doctor, to our questioning your servant?'

'Certainly not, sir! He is an Austrian. Oscar Prantz is his name, and he has been with me for years. He admits all visitors and nothing could happen in this house without his knowledge. Would you like to see him at once or will you wait?'

'I would like to see him now,' said the detective.

'Very well, Mr. Quest.'

The pressure of an electric bell brought the servant to the library. He came in quietly, with an expression on his face that would have done credit to the stiffest of old family butlers. He looked across at his master.

'This gentleman wishes to put some questions to you, Prantz,' said the doctor. 'I need not tell you to be perfectly truthful with him.'

Oscar Prantz turned to the detective.

'What do you wish to know, sir?' he asked.

'To begin with,' said Quest, 'how long have you been with Dr. Burgin?'

'For nearly sixteen years, sir.'

'Without a break?'

'Without a break, sir.'

'Where were you living when the doctor engaged you?'

'I was in Vienna at the time.'

'Have you ever lived with him in Paris?'

'I have not, sir.'

'Have you ever been to Paris?'

'No, sir, I have never been there in my life.'

'Dr. Burgin was there eight or nine years ago.'

'Yes, sir, I remember. He went from Prague to Paris on a visit, but I did not accompany him. I was allowed a holiday and went to visit my relatives in Vienna.'

Quest looked at him steadily for a minute and then said: '

'Did a gentleman call at this house any time during the evening of last Monday.'

'Nobody called that evening, or that

night, or during the day.'

'Are you sure?'

'Quite sure, sir. It is very seldom the doctor has a visitor.'

'Did you ever hear of a Frenchman by the name of Pierre Renault?'

'No, sir. The name is not familiar to me.'

'By the way, did Dr. Burgin tell you yesterday that I might call again and question you?'

'No, sir. I don't even know who you are.'

'Thank you, Prantz. That will be all,' said Quest, and watched him as he left the room.

When he had gone Quest suggested that they should begin the search. They started with the ground floor — there was no cellar and no basement — and mounted to the other floors, going into every room.

They glanced into a large bathroom, and entered a laboratory that was equipped with analytical appliances, many of which were strange to Quest. And everywhere they went Dr. Burgin opened cupboards and wardrobes and even several trunks, and with a stick he had brought with him, tapped the walls to show that there were no hollow spaces behind them.

He gave them every facility, and when they had finished and descended the stairs he took them out into the garden. They searched it as thoroughly as they had searched the house, peering into the clumps of shrubbery and examining every yard of ground to see if the earth had been disturbed.

'Thank you, Doctor,' said Quest, when they had finished. 'I hope we have not put you to any inconvenience?'

There was a suspicion of a sneer on Dr. Burgin's face.

'Not at all, sir,' he replied amiably. 'I am very glad you have made the search. Perhaps now you will believe that I had no hand in the disappearance of your friend.'

'We did not doubt you, Dr. Burgin,' replied Quest. 'But we felt it would be best to make absolutely sure that no suspicion could rest on you.'

'I quite understand, Mr. Quest. I have no ill feeling. You have only done your duty.'

Dr. Burgin said good-bye to them at the gate and returned to the house, and Quest and Robert Ferris walked along the Grove and picked up a taxi at the corner.

'In spite of the fact that we found nothing,' said Robert Ferris as they drove along, 'I don't suppose you have changed your mind. I haven't, I can assure you.'

'Nor have I,' declared the detective. 'I am still firmly convinced that the doctor has had a hand in the disappearance of Renault. In fact I'll go so far as to say that he has murdered him!'

'But — but what can he have done with the body?'

'I don't know,' said Philip Quest. 'Very likely it's floating in the Thames.'

They were both silent for a few minutes and then Ferris suddenly spoke.

'What did you think of that servant, Quest?'

'He's a shrewd and cunning rascal. I didn't expect him to tell me anything different. I questioned him only to see if I could throw him off his guard, but he didn't turn a hair.'

'Probably well coached by Burgin,' said

Ferris. 'They are a pair of scoundrels. We shall have our work cut out to get to the bottom of them — at least you will. I shall be too busy to help you much. You will take it on?'

'You can leave it to me,' said the detective.

'I have no intention of dropping it now.'

'It's going to be a hard job,' said the Scotland Yard man. 'How can you get at the doctor? He can't be arrested for there's actually nothing against him.'

'No, he's clever. Whatever has happened he's covered it up so well that he can't be touched. But somehow or other I'm going to find a way to get at him.'

'How?'

'I don't know. I'll come round to the Yard tomorrow and talk it over with you.'

'Very well, and I'll lend you a couple of my best men if you like.'

Quest did not answer. He was silent for a few moments, and once or twice he frowned and shook his head.

'I don't know what to make of Dr. Francis Burgin,' he remarked at length. He baffles me. Two things I noticed when we were searching the house.'

'What were they?' asked Robert Ferris.

'The laboratory was most extensively equipped. There were several appliances of which I have no knowledge, and also the tub in the bathroom. It was uncommonly large and deep for one thing, and though it looked to be quite a new one, I noticed that the porcelain interior of it was slightly corroded in places.'

'There's nothing significant about that, is there?'

'Maybe not, and yet — '

The taxi stopped in front of the detective's offices in the City, and he got out. Robert Ferris drove on, and Quest entered the office door and went straight through to the consulting room. Here he found his partner, Richard Lester, and told him briefly of the visit to Dr. Burgin.

'At present I don't know what I shall do,' he said when he had finished. 'I'll think it over tonight and try and come to some decision. But of one thing I am certain. Pierre Renault is dead and Dr. Francis Burgin knows all about it!'

4

The House in Shadwell

'From information which was received yesterday the police have been led to believe that they will shortly arrest one of the two men who were concerned in the mysterious affair at the Rising Sun public house at Wapping some time ago, when an attempt was made to steal a corpse that had been taken from the river.'

★　★　★

Philip Quest read this paragraph in the paper while he was at breakfast on the morning after his second visit to Dr. Burgin, and shortly after he was on his way to Scotland Yard with the paper in his pocket. He was not going to call on Robert Ferris, however, he would see him after he had made enquiries in another quarter.

Arriving at the big building on the Embankment he went straight up to Inspector Johnson's room, and finding him there showed the paragraph to him.

'Have you read this?' he said.

The Inspector nodded.

'Yes,' he replied. 'Is this what brought you here?'

'It is,' said Quest. 'I'd like to have some information.'

'I didn't know you were interested in the Wapping affair.'

'I am, very much, as it happens.'

'You would be, Quest. You are always stumbling on something. In this instance I suppose you don't agree with the police theory that the men who tried to carry off the body from the public house wanted to sell it for dissection?'

'I am quite sure, my dear fellow, that they had no such motive.'

Inspector Johnson shrugged his shoulders and smiled sceptically.

'I won't agree with you,' he said. 'It would be useless. However, you can have the information you want. It appears that a man by the name of Alf Thomas, a labourer in the East End, saw a car with two men in it near the Rising Sun on the night of the crime, and recognised one of them as Larry Smith, who is, as you know, a crook of the lowest type.

'The same night Alf Thomas was knocked down by a cab and seriously injured and was taken to hospital. He was there for some time and it was not until he was discharged yesterday that he learned of the Wapping affair. He went at once to the Wapping police station and told his story to the detective-sergeant. The sergeant telephoned through to the Yard and the matter was put in my hands.'

'And Larry Smith has been arrested?' asked Quest.

'No — not yet. The Wapping police did not know where he lived, neither did Alf Thomas.'

'This news should not have been allowed to leak out, Johnson. How did it happen?'

'That I don't know. Somebody must have talked too freely. It is very unfortunate, for in all likelihood Larry

Smith has been warned of his danger and is lying low. That paragraph appeared in the paper last evening as well as the morning paper you have.'

'You are leaving the search to the Wapping police, I suppose?' asked Quest.

The Inspector shook his head.

'No,' he answered. 'I sent one of my men, Tom Grey, to the East End last night. I haven't heard from him yet so he must still be making enquiries. I don't suppose it will be long before he gets on Larry Smith's trail.'

'I have my doubts,' said the detective. 'From what I know of Smith he's a very wary bird. It will not be easy for Grey to — '

He broke off and laughed.

'What's the joke?' asked Johnson. 'What are you laughing at?'

'At your camouflage. Since you have sent Tom Grey to find Smith it is quite obvious that you regard the Rising Sun affair as something more important than an attempt to steal a corpse for dissection. Am I right?'

'All right, Quest. I might just as well

own up. I do. At first I didn't believe so, but I have come to the conclusion that there may be something deep at the bottom of it — '

'So there is,' broke in Philip Quest. 'It's not an ordinary case of body-snatching. When this mystery is cleared up — '

The telephone on the desk rang, the inspector attended to it and carried on a short conversation.

'That was Tom Grey,' he said, when he had rung off. 'He didn't give me any particulars, but he has learned from somebody where Larry Smith is living. He's waiting at the Railway Station in Keble Street, and I'm going over. Would you like to come, too?'

'Yes, I should,' Quest answered. 'I was going to see Ferris this morning, but that can wait.'

They were soon on their way, and in the taxi talked of the Wapping mystery and wondered what information they could get from the little crook. At Keble Street Tom Grey was waiting, and they dismissed the cab and joined him. As they walked he told them all he knew.

'I've had a long search,' he said. 'At first I talked with a lot of people who swore they had never heard of Larry Smith, but at last somebody put me on to one of his girl friends. I questioned her and she told me all I wanted to know. She had been very friendly with Smith but it appears they quarrelled and she had a grudge against him. She told me where he was living, Number 81, Vicar's Lane, Shadwell, on the top floor of the house, in a room opposite to the head of the stairs. I know the place, I've been there. Rusty Burns, who was released from Pentonville last week, lives in the house, also on the top floor. At least, he did before he went 'inside'.'

'I know the place,' said Inspector Johnson. 'It's a positive nest of crooks. I wonder if we'll find Smith at Home?'

'I should think so,' replied Tom Grey. 'If he read that paragraph in the paper he's been lying low, afraid to put his nose out of doors.'

They had turned from Keble Street into Vicar's Lane, and a few more yards brought them to Number 81, a rickety old tenement house. Quietly they ascended the four flights of stairs and stopped at a door across from the top landing. It was locked. The Inspector rapped, and rapped again, but there was no response. Not a sound could be heard from within. Quest stooped and looked through the keyhole.

'The key isn't in the lock,' he said, 'and all I can see is a window.'

'He must be out,' said Tom Grey. 'We'll have to wait until he returns, or — '

As he spoke a door on the other side of the passage was opened and Rusty Burns appeared, a lean, lantern-jawed youth, with red hair. He grinned at the little group.

'My word, all Scotland Yard to arrest poor old Larry! Has he robbed the Bank of England or stole the Crown Jewels?'

'We don't want any of your impudence, Burns!' snapped Tom Grey. 'What do you know about Larry Smith? Where has he gone?'

'He hasn't gone anywhere,' Rusty Burns replied.

'He isn't in his room.'

'He must be. I've been sitting in my own room since I got up this morning, at seven, and I haven't heard Larry go out. I've been expecting him to come in and have a bit of breakfast with me, he said he would.'

'When did he tell you?'

'Early last evening.'

'Have you heard him moving about today,' continued Tom Grey.

'No. Haven't heard a sound,' replied the youth.

'Has he been keeping to his room?'

'Yes, since yesterday afternoon, when he read something in the paper that frightened him. He said he was afraid the police would be looking for him, and he dare not show his face in the street.'

Inspector Johnson rapped once more on the door, but in vain.

'He must have cleared out during the night,' he said.

'Let us make sure before we go,' said the detective. 'Lend a hand.'

Hurling their weight against the door the three of them burst it open in one effort.

'My God!' said Tom Grey, in a low voice.

Larry Smith lay on a shabby couch, his legs dangling to the floor. He was quite dead. On his forehead was a wound that was clotted with blood, made by some blunt instrument. The expression on his face was calm. The blow must have killed him instantly, and at the moment when he was struck down he could not have been in any fear of his assailant.

There were no signs of a struggle in the cheaply furnished little room. The bed had not been slept in. On the table stood a beer bottle, a glass, and a packet of cigarettes.

Rusty Burns, who had followed the others in, was staring in horror at the body, his features twitching.

'Poor old Larry!' he muttered.

'This is a queer business, Grey,' said the Inspector.

Tom Grey nodded.

'It certainly is,' he replied. 'Somebody had a nasty grievance against Smith. It couldn't have been one of his pals, he never squealed on them.'

'I know that,' said the Inspector. 'Whoever the murderer was he wasn't in a hurry to get away. He's taken the weapon, and when he left he locked the door and took the key out.'

Philip Quest had nothing to say. He was very disappointed. He had hoped the Larry Smith would throw some light on the affair at the Rising Sun, and now —

He had his own idea as to why the little crook had been murdered and who had killed him. But he had no intention of telling the others. He would keep that to himself, and for the strongest reason. There had suddenly flashed to his mind a theory which, though rather weak, was to some extent plausible, because of two things he had recalled in connection with the second case of body-snatching.

There were no finger-prints, either. The assassin had been too clever to leave any. Inspector Johnson made a futile search and then turned to Rusty Burns.

'What do you know of this?' he asked sternly.

'Me, sir?' exclaimed the youth. 'I don't know nothing about. I swear I don't!'

'You ought to know something about it. Your room is just across the passage.'

'All I know is that Larry Smith had a visitor last night.'

'A visitor? Why didn't you tell us this before?'

'I didn't think of it, Inspector.'

'Well, think about it now!' snapped Inspector Johnson. 'Did you see this person?'

'No,' answered Rusty Burns.

'What time did he arrive?'

'It was about eleven o'clock when I heard him come quietly up the stairs and give a funny sort of knock on Larry's door. Larry let him in at once. I heard their voices for a few minutes and then I must have dropped off to sleep.'

'You didn't hear this visitor leave?'

'No, Inspector.'

'Did you hear any of the conversation?'

'Not a clear word, sir. They were talking very low.'

'Do you think they were quarrelling, Burns?'

'I couldn't say. They never once raised their voices. I supposed the man was some pal of Larry's.'

'You have no idea who he might have been?'

'No, sir, I haven't. Larry had a lot of friends.'

Inspector Johnson was satisfied, and so was Tom Grey. This young crook could not have had any motive for the crime, and apart from his petty thieving he hadn't a bad record.

His statements had cleared up a few points. Some persons who knew Larry Smith well had called on him late on the previous night, had talked to him quietly, and then suddenly murdered him, taking him by surprise.

The Inspector turned to Philip Quest.

'There can be little doubt,' he said, 'that the murderer is the man who was Larry Smith's accomplice in the attempt to steal the body from the Rising Sun. He must have read the paragraph in the paper and knowing that Smith was likely to be arrested killed him before he had time to talk.'

'It's a very plausible theory,' Quest assented, voicing his own belief.

'And yet that isn't of much value. We haven't been able to get the faintest clue to the identity of this man.'

'No, that's unfortunate,' said Quest.

'We'll have a hard job to trace him,' went on the Inspector. 'He has a car, and it's my conviction that he was some person from the West End who hired Smith to assist him.'

The detective nodded in agreement.

They searched in the dead man's pockets but discovered nothing that could throw any light on the murder. They talked with Rusty Burns again, but he could tell them no more than he already had.

'There's something else I want to ask you, Burns,' said Philip Quest. 'You know about the Rising Sun affair, I suppose?'

'I read about it in the papers, sir,' replied Burns.

'Did Larry Smith tell you he had been concerned in it?'

'No, he didn't. He was always very close about any 'job' he had done, even with his best pals.'

'You have no idea who this other man could be?'

'I can't guess, Mr. Quest. It was only five or six days ago that Larry came to live in Vicar's Lane, and since then the only visitor he has had was the one what come last night.'

During this questioning Tom Grey had been searching the room and he was now at the bed. He lifted up the mattress and took from beneath it a thin, flat parcel, wrapped in paper. This he tore open and displayed to view a sheaf of Bank of England notes. He counted them rapidly.

'H'm! Seventy-five pounds!' he exclaimed.

'It's the money Smith was paid for helping to steal the body at Wapping,' declared Inspector Johnson. 'This alters the look of things,' he went on, throwing a suspicious look at Rusty Burns. 'It seems to me that Smith was killed by some pal of his who knew the money was in his possession.'

Philip Quest smiled.

'That is ridiculous,' he said.

'Ridiculous? Why?'

'I'll tell you why, Johnson. The murderer was in no hurry to leave, and, therefore, had robbery been the motive for the crime, he would have searched and found the notes.'

'H'm! Yes, yes — you're right, Quest,' admitted the Inspector.

The discovery of the money was, in Philip Quest's opinion, another small link in the chain of deductions he had previously formed.

He did not stay any longer. He left the room, remarking to Johnson that he had something important to attend to. A taxi from Keble Street Station took him to Scotland Yard, where he had a long interview with Robert Ferris.

It was nearly two hours later when he arrived at his offices and found Richard Lester eagerly awaiting him for news. He told him all that had happened, and then, armed with a box of cigarettes, settled himself in his favourite armchair. For half an hour he sat there, smoking cigarette after cigarette, and Richard Lester waited, knowing that eventually his senior partner would tell him of his theories.

'I've been working this out,' he said at length, 'and I think I've hit on something.

Let's take the murder of Smith at Shadwell, first. I think we can assume, beyond any doubt, that the guilty party is the man who was Larry Smith's accomplice in the Rising Sun affair. He saw the paragraph in the paper yesterday and it alarmed him. Satisfied that somebody had put the police on Smith's track, and fearing that if he was arrested he would own up, he went to the house in Vicar's Lane last night and murdered the poor fellow.'

'That's logical,' said Lester. 'Go on.'

'Now, here are some points, or rather facts, that are very striking,' Quest resumed. 'There was a sum of seventy-five pounds in Larry Smith's possession. This money must have been paid to him by his accomplice. Now, Dr. Burgin is in prosperous cicumstances. He could easily have afforded to — '

'Good Heavens! You're not suggesting — '

'Don't interrupt. Let me finish. You remember that the man whom Smith helped to steal the body at Wapping wore a very long mask. That was obviously to

56

conceal a beard or moustache, or at least a beard, and Dr. Burgin has a large moustache and a flowing beard. The next point is this. The car from which the hamper, containing the stolen body was flung into the road turned into Circus Road after it had passed me, and that is the route it would have taken if it had been going to St. John's Wood.

'And now for the fourth and last point. Assuming that my deductions are correct, Dr. Burgin would, sooner or later, have tried to steal another body. But there has been no such attempt. Why? Because the French detective, Pierre Renault, fell into the doctor's hands. If that is so, my hypothetical case has been clearly established.'

Richard Lester's face was flushed with excitement.

'It looks as if you are right!' he exclaimed. 'I'm beginning to believe that it was Dr. Burgin who tried to steal the corpse from the Samaritan Hospital and got away with one from the pub at Wapping!'

'I am very much inclined to believe so

myself,' assented Quest. 'There is no certainty, of course.'

'What could Dr. Burgin have wanted a human body for? I can't understand that.'

'Neither can I. It's a mystery, and a very unwholesome one, too.'

'Well, we've got a difficult task in front of us — that is if you mean to go on with it.'

There was a steely light in Philip Quest's eyes.

'Go on with it?' he repeated in a hard voice. 'Certainly I am. We are going to watch Dr. Burgin, shadow him wherever he goes. We are going to find the secret of that house in St. John's Wood, and one day Lester, we'll put a rope round the neck of Dr. Burgin!'

5

The Fight in the Wood

The affairs of the Samaritan Hospital, the Rising Sun public-house, and the murder in Vicar's Lane were forgotten by the public. And also the strange disappearance of the French detective, which had got into the papers. Pierre Renault was dead, doubtless the victim of a cruel murder, and his secret was buried with him, if he was buried.

The police were doing nothing to solve any of the crimes, for there was nothing to be done. They had tried to find the murderer of Larry Smith, but had been forced to drop their investigations.

Robert Ferris, busy with the tasks imposed on him at Scotland Yard, had no time to spare in attempting to unravel the mystery of his vanished friend.

But Philip Quest and his partner were not idle. Working patiently, and with great care, they were dogging Dr. Burgin's footsteps, haunting him like shadows, determined to spare no efforts to bring him to justice, and hoping to be successful.

The Countess of Mere, one of London's most popular hostesses, gave a reception one night at her house in Grosvenor Square. The house was a blaze of light. Outside a strip of carpet was stretched across the pavement beneath a striped awning, and guests were continually arriving, stared at by the usual crowd of admiring spectators.

Within the big house an orchestra was playing and servants in livery were moving to and fro among the numerous guests, many of whom were persons of fame and distinction, for the reception, given annually by the Countess, was one of the big events of the season.

A striking figure, even in this brilliant assemblage, was a tall, very handsome man of middle age, who was obviously a foreigner; a slim, graceful man, immaculately dressed, with an olive tinted complexion, aristocratic features, a small black moustache, and a slender beard, cut to a point, thick, raven black hair that had a tendency to curl, and dark, piercing eyes. Had he worn Spanish attire of the seventeenth century he might have stepped from a canvas painted by Velasquez.

Looking somewhat bored, he strolled about, nodding to no friend or acquaintance, unrecognised by any of the gathering.

He made his way through the crowded ballroom, crossed a passage, and went into the conservatory. At the same instant a man who was sitting there, smoking a cigar, rose to his feet. A tall man of powerful build, with a pallid complexion, a heavy black moustache, and a beard that flowed to his chest.

'Peter!' he said, in a low, sharp tone. 'Peter!'

The other gave a quick start.

'You are mistaken, sir,' he replied.

'Surely not. You have changed, yet not so much that I can have made a mistake.'

'My name is Ramenez — Juan Ramenez.'

'What's in a name? I knew you years ago in Cuba, in Rome, Vienna. You haven't forgotten me, my friend. Look closer.'

The young man stepped a pace nearer. 'Daryak!' he exclaimed.

'Not so loud,' said the other. 'That name belongs to the old days. I am Dr. Francis Burgin now. And so you are Peter, the sharer of my wandering life.'

They shook hands warmly, and moving to a couch among the potted shrubs, sat down side by side. For a few seconds they were silent while memories of the past crowded into their minds. They had been comrades once, knit together by such a bond as often unites those who live by their wits, and each knew that the other's friendship could be relied on.

For some little time they talked, and then Burgin suggested that they should move.

'We had better separate, it is not wise to be seen together.'

The two withdrew from the conservatory, and a few moments later a tall figure in evening-dress entered the house from the garden at the rear of it.

Avoiding the guests as much as possible, he went to the cloakroom for his hat and overcoat, strolled along the hall and passed out of the big house into Grosvenor Square. It was Philip Quest, and how he came to be at the reception is easily explained.

Lester, watching the house in Lime Grove, had shadowed the Doctor from there to the Countess of Mere's reception, and had 'phoned this news to Quest who was at the office. Without delay the detective had got into evening-dress and taken a taxi to Mere House. He had not been stopped, though he had no invitation. He had gone calmly in — a thing which is often and easily done at large receptions — in fact he had gate-crashed. After wandering about for a while he had seen Dr. Burgin enter the conservatory, and had subsequently seen him joined there by Juan Ramenez.

He had then slipped out to the garden and listened by the side of the conservatory in the hope of hearing the conversation. To his disappointment, however, he had not been able to hear much. When Dr. Burgin and his companion had separated he had gone home, and in the comfort of the consulting room had told Richard Lester what had occurred.

'Unfortunately I learned very little,' he continued after speaking of his attempt to listen in the garden. 'What meagre information I did get is interesting, though. The two men must have been intimate friends in the past, and at that time, it would seem, Dr. Burgin used the name of Daryak. It was in that name he was addressed by his companion, and he called the other Ramenez. They talked mostly in low tones, but at intervals I caught little bits of their conversation.

'It appears that Dr. Burgin has a country house somewhere in Essex, not far from London. He is taking Ramenez down there tomorrow, and they are to meet at Liverpool Street at five in the afternoon. They will travel by rail to Durling Wood, and a car belonging to the doctor will be waiting for them at the station.'

'Anything else?' asked his young partner.

'No, that is all I could gather.'

'I suppose you are going to do something?'

'Certainly. It is just possible that this information will be the opening thrust for a wedge for us. It may even lead to the arrest of Burgin and his companion for the murder of Pierre Renault. I must have some enquiries made about Remenez. I dare say he is well known in the West End, since he was one of the Countess of Mere's invited guests.'

'Or an uninvited one,' suggested Lester.

The detective shook his head.

'I think not,' he said. 'I think he must have received an invitation, and the doctor also. Which means they must each have at least one friend in high society.'

'Well, what am I to do?'

'I think you had better go down to Durling Wood by an earlier train tomorrow afternoon, and wait until the doctor and his friend arrive. Try and find out where they are going and have a look at the house — I want to know exactly where it is — and anything more you can learn. You had better take your bicycle down with you, and for goodness sake be careful. Remember it is no ordinary criminal we are dealing with. I don't doubt that Dr. Burgin has been on his guard since I paid the second visit to him with Robert Ferris. Possibly he knows his movements are being watched. I shouldn't be surprised if he does.'

Philip Quest paused while he lighted another cigarette.

'I don't often make a mistake in character, Lester,' he went on. 'Most criminals have some flaw in their armour, and if my judgment is correct Dr. Burgin has at least one weakness, and that is self-conceit. I am sure he has lived by his wits for years, and has probably never once fallen into the hands of the police. That alone would have given him an exaggerated sense of security, and watchful though he may be, I think he will take risks in the arrogant belief that he will have nothing to fear. If he does, we shall have him in the end.'

On the following afternoon Richard Lester went down to Essex, taking his bicycle with him, by a train that left Liverpool Street at three o'clock. Obeying instructions from Quest he travelled on to the station past Durling Wood, and from there cycled the five miles back to the little village. He stopped at the Farmer's Inn, entered the tap room, and seated himself on a bench by the window that overlooked the railway station, which was some hundred yards beyond the village. He had not more than half an hour to wait, and by the time he had finished sandwiches and a drink, a saloon car, driven by a red faced man, who had the appearance of a farm-labourer, stopped alongside of the station.

And shortly after the train for which he had been waiting came in. Dr. Burgin and his companion descended from it, each carrying a small bag, and when they had stepped into the car, the chauffeur swung it round and drove away by a cross road that ran eastward.

The young woman who had served him came to the window to see the arrival of the train, and Lester, wanting information started a conversation with her.

'There was something familiar about the gentleman who has gone off in that car, I mean the one with the black beard. I believe I have seen him in London,' he said carelessly.

'I dare say you have,' answered the woman. 'He lives in Town. That is Mr. Edward Charning.'

'Charning, eh? He looks like a foreigner, so does the man with him.'

'I don't know who he is, sir. It is the first time I've seen him down here. Mr. Charning comes now and again for the weekend. He has a place in the country, over towards the sea. Doomesday House it's called. He bought it two or three years ago.'

'Doomesday House!' repeated Lester. 'That's a queer name.'

'It's a queer sort of place,' said the woman. 'I've been by it once or twice. The story goes that it is haunted by the ghost of a murdered man.'

'I shouldn't think servants would stay there long then.'

'There is only one servant. The man Hodge, who drives the car.'

'It sounds very interesting. I'd like to have a look at Doomesday House, if it isn't far out of my way.'

'It's about five miles from here. Take the first turn to the left by the station and keep straight on. You will pass a couple of farms and some cottages, and then there isn't another house until you come to Mr. Charning's, a mile and a half further. It stands to the left of the road.'

Richard Lester did not ask any more questions, he paid for what he had had and left the inn. When he had walked his bicycle as far as the crossroads he stopped in hesitation.

He was inclined to return to Town, but, remembering that Quest had told him to take a look at the house, he mounted his machine and pedalled to the East.

'I'll learn what I can,' he said to himself. 'An old house with no other dwelling near! And Dr. Burgin bought it in the name of Charning! It's all very mysterious.'

Riding fast he presently passed the farms and the cottages, and as he went on, with the salty air of the sea blowing in his face, the country grew more desolate. As far as the eye could see were only clumps of woods, stretches of flat marshland, winding streams fringed with stinted willows, and here and there an abandoned windmill.

Evening shadows were falling when Lester saw in front of him, to the left, the roof of a house that was buried amongst trees.

On both sides of him were plantations. Here he dismounted and hid his bicycle in a thicket to the right of the road, then walked cautiously on, keeping to the wooded cover, until be was directly opposite to the grounds of Doomesday House.

He could see a pair of wooden gates set in a high hedge, and that was all. The roof of the house was no longer visible, it was hidden by the trees. He picked up a heavy stick of wood — he had an idea that it might come in useful — and waited for a while; and finally, when it was quite dark, he glided to the other side of the road.

Finding the gates locked he moved along the hedge until he saw a small gap, and succeeded in squeezing through it. He was inside the grounds, and near to the gravel drive.

He avoided that and stole cautiously forward in the shelter of trees and shrubbery, pausing occasionally to listen. He had advanced for about fifty yards, and suddenly he came to an open strip of lawn, and had a clear view of the house.

It looked sombre and repellent in the darkness. Only one light was visible, and that was at a curtained window on the ground floor.

Faintly to his ears came the murmur of conversation. On a balcony that projected above the door could be seen the outline of two figures, and two glowing red spots. Dr. Burgin and his companion were sitting up there, talking and smoking. For a few minutes Lester stood at the edge of the lawn, trying vainly to hear the conversation; and at length, when he was about to shift his position, one of the speakers said distinctly, in a petulant voice:

'I don't like it, Burgin! I wish you wouldn't suggest it! I'm a pretty bad lot, but hang it all, I'm not such a callous devil as you are! Cold blooded murder isn't in my line! If it was anything else — '

'Not so loud, my dear fellow!'

Richard Lester's heart was throbbing with excitement. This was important. He must try to hear more. How could he? He crept through the shrubbery, parellel with the lawn, with the intention of making a detour that would bring him beneath the balcony.

But he had gone no more than a yard or so when his ankle came in contact with a taut wire, and at the same time he heard a bell ring violently in the house.

He had fallen into a trap that had been set for intruders, and had started an alarm.

'There's somebody in the grounds!' exclaimed Dr. Burgin looking over the balcony as he spoke. 'Hodge! Hodge! Where are you, Hodge?'

'Coming, sir,' a voice answered from below.

'Hurry! Don't let him get away, Hodge! Shoot if you have to!'

The servant was hastening towards the spot where the wire was stretched. For a second Lester had been too startled to move, and now, as he got a glimpse of the man and heard Burgin's instructions, he took to his heels.

He ran like a deer to the bottom of the garden, somehow got through the hedge, darted across the road, and plunged into the plantation on the opposite side, knowing that he would not have time to get his bicycle.

His only chance was to elude his pursuer, but he soon found that he could not do this, and as he tore blindly on, crashing loudly among the thicket, he heard the servant drawing nearer.

A couple of pistol shots were fired at him, and the bullets hummed close to his ears. An inspiration flashed to his mind. He still had the stick, and suddenly, as a third shot grazed his shoulder, he stopped short, and slipped behind a tree. He crouched there, and a few seconds later, as the servant came running within reach of him, he let fly the piece of wood.

The man was taken unawares. The blow landed on his head with considerable force and staggered him.

He was not put out of action, though. Dazed as he was, he made a reeling leap at Lester, and seized him by the throat.

The two fell, and there was a desperate struggle. But it did not last long, for the man, Hodge, had been severely injured by the blow, and without his pistol which he must have dropped in the fight, he could not make much of a show.

His strenuous efforts soon ceased, and he had to let go of the young man, who scrambled to his feet and took to his heels again.

Only a brief interval had elapsed since the watcher had sprung the alarm. Voices could now be heard and the gleam of a lantern danced amidst the trees. Dr. Burgin and his guest were approaching, coming to search for the servant.

Lester gave them a wide berth. He had a rough idea of his bearings, and when he had worked stealthily round through the woods for some distance he stumbled on the road at a point close to where he had hidden his bicycle. He had no intention of departing yet, however. He knew it would be unsafe, for he had no doubt that they would still be searching for him.

'He might suspect that I was sent down here by Quest,' he reflected, 'and in that case they are sure to scour the place for me.'

He worked his way round until he was almost opposite the gates of Doomesday House, and stretched himself flat on the ground, in the shelter of a clump of bushes.

Presently he saw Dr. Burgin and his guest appear from the woods nearby with the servant, who was walking unsteadily, with their assistance.

They led him across to the gateway and up the drive, and then, shortly afterwards they re-appeared in the car, without the servant, and turned in the direction of Durling Wood.

Lester prudently remained where he

was. He waited nearly an hour, and it was not until the car had returned and he had seen the gates shut and locked that he left his hiding place and stole away to get his bicycle.

He did not go to Durling Wood station, but rode to a station nearer Town, got a train from there to Liverpool Street, and reached home soon after ten o'clock.

Philip Quest was just having supper; he, too, he explained, had been out all the evening. Lester sat down at the table, and while he ate the very welcome food, told his story to the detective, who listened in silence until it was finished. His face was very grave.

'You ran a big risk,' he said. 'If you had been caught I should never have seen you alive again. And some harm has been done. It is obvious, now, that Burgin will suspect that I sent you to Doomesday House. If this is so, and believing that I have made the first move, he may attempt to strike back. Anyway,' he said kindly, 'the information you got is worth the risk you took.'

'I wish I had been able to hear more of

their conversation on the balcony,' said Lester.

'Yes, it's a great pity you couldn't,' replied Quest. 'We are entirely in the dark as to the identity of Dr. Burgin's intended victim. All we know is that he proposes to murder somebody, presumably for gain, and that Juan Ramenez — '

'Juan Ramenez? How did you find out his name?'

'I learned that today, but let me finish. I was about to say that Ramenez has been urged to assist, and that, since he spoke of the doctor's proposal being a temptation, the murder would clearly be to his profit, too. And yet he is reluctant to have anything to do with it.'

'I daresay he will consent in the end, though.'

'I expect he will. By his own admission he is a pretty bad lot, as I supposed.'

'Is that the kind of report you got of him?' asked the young man.

Philip Quest shook his head.

'On the contrary,' he answered. 'I made enquiries of a number of persons, several of them members of my club; and the information I received from authoritative sources amounts to this. Juan Rameniz is a cultured man of about forty-five. He speaks three or four languages, and is believed to belong to an old and titled Spanish family of Castille. He came to London a month ago — for the first time, I believe — and took expensive chambers in St. James's. He brought with him letters of introduction from some prominent person living in Madrid and Seville, and through these letters he got a footing in West End society. He has been admitted to the membership of a club in Pall Mall, and the few friends he has made have a high opinion of him.'

'That doesn't fit with what we know about him.'

'Not in the least,' said the detective. 'He is a wolf in sheeps' clothing, right enough, and I'll bet as big a rascal as Dr. Francis Burgin.'

Quest had finished his supper. He left the table and settled himself in front of the fire, and while he smoked there was a frown on his face.

'We've got to try and stop this

contemplated murder,' he said, after a pause. 'But it's going to be very difficult. I don't think it would help to bother much with Ramenez, at present, we'll drop him, and keep a close watch on Burgin. That's all we can do for the time being.'

6

A Chain of Mysteries

Had Philip Quest not been a man of unlimited patience and perseverance, he might have washed his hands of the difficult task he had undertaken and handed the whole affair over to Scotland Yard.

More than two weeks had gone by, and nothing had been achieved. The surveillance of Dr. Burgin had yielded no results. His residence in St. John's Wood had been closely watched. On several occasions he had managed to give either Lester or Quest the slip when he went out, and they had then lost track of him for several hours. He had paid two brief visits to the house in Essex, accompanied by Juan Ramenez, and occasionally he and Ramenez had lunched and dined together in some restaurant in Town.

There was every reason to believe that

they were contemplating the murder of some unknown person, but if so, they were in no hurry to carry out their plans.

Such was the unsatisfactory state of affairs when one evening, while Lester was on duty in Grove Road, and Philip Quest was sitting idle at home, the maid brought him a card that bore the name of Carol Renoff.

The name was unfamiliar to him. He hesitated, and then told the servant that he would see the visitor. A few moments later there came into the consulting room a very beautiful girl, fashionably dressed, with dark hair and eyes. She was obviously very nervous.

'I am very sorry to intrude like this, Mr. Quest,' she said. 'But I am so very worried.'

'You are in trouble, Miss Renoff? But how can I help?'

'It is not on my account,' was the answer. 'Mr. Quest, you do take private cases, don't you?'

'Occasionally,' said Quest modestly, and wondering what on earth could have brought this beautiful person to see him.

'Oh, I'm so glad,' said Carol Renoff. 'Please, may I speak to you in confidence?'

'Certainly. You can take that for granted,' smiled the detective.

'Then I will tell you everything. I don't want David to know I have been here. He forbade me to come. I begged him to consult you or go to the police, and he refused to do either. He doesn't seem to realise that he ought — '

Her sudden rush of words stopped, and she smiled weakly at Quest.

'I beg your pardon, Mr. Quest, but it is such a relief to know that I can tell you about things that I'm afraid I forgot to explain.'

'Don't worry,' said Philip Quest. 'Take your time. But won't you sit down?'

He indicated a chair by the fire, and when she was seated he handed her the cigarette box. She took one, and lighted it, as did Quest. In a few moments she seemed more at her ease. The nervous excitement left her face.

'I had better explain myself,' she said. 'I am Polish, and at present I live in

Cresswell Road with my father. He prefers England to his own country. I have been engaged for some time to David Morley. You probably know who he is.'

'I think so,' said the detective. 'He is the son of the late Gerald Morley, the millionaire.'

'Yes, the only son, and the last of the family. His father died some years ago, leaving him a great deal of money and a large house in Beverly Street. He is twenty-six years old now. A very nice man and very popular.'

'I have seen him often, Miss Renoff. He impressed me as being a very sensible young man.'

'He is generous and kind-hearted. It is impossible to think of any person wishing to do him harm, and yet — '

The girl's voice faltered. She paused, with a look of distress in her eyes, and Quest waited until she had her feelings under control.

'It is a most amazing story,' she went on. 'Three mysterious things have happened. It began about two weeks ago, when David was crossing Beverly Street late at night. He had nearly got to the pavement and a closed car was approaching behind him, in the middle of the road. He was not in the way, but the chauffeur suddenly swerved and drove straight at him. It was a deliberate attempt to run David down, and he would have been killed if he had not been quick to leap to one side. As it was the car grazed him.'

'And dashed on?' enquired Quest.

'Yes, it didn't stop. It swung back to the middle of the road and disappeared in the direction of Piccadilly.'

'There can be no doubt that the chauffeur swerved with the intention of running him down?'

'David was certain that he did. It was a dry night and the car could not have skidded.'

'I suppose Mr. Morley did not notice the number of the car?'

'No. He said it happened too quickly.'

Quest's interest was roused.

'Go on,' he said. 'What was the next occurrence?'

'That happened at the end of last

week,' replied Carol Renoff, 'and again at night. David had walked from his club in St. James's Street, and just as he reached his house a closed car — apparently the same one — stopped several yards behind him, and he saw three men jump out of it and hurry towards him. At that moment the butler was just leaving the house to post a letter, and David darted inside, and shut and locked the door barely in time. The men did not come any further than the porch. They got hastily back in the car and drove away. It was too dark for David to see them distinctly, and he could not say what they looked like.'

'And when did the third mystery occur?'

'Three days ago,' said the girl. 'During the evening, when David was at dinner, he received a letter by district messenger from a friend of his who lives in St. James's, saying he had been taken ill and wished to see him as soon as possible. David left the house at once, and as there was not a taxi to be had, he walked. He was passing a dark spot at the bottom of Beverly Street when somebody struck him a blow on the head from behind. When he came to his senses he was at home, lying on a couch in the library. He had been picked up and carried to his house by two constables, who knew who he was. They told him they had seen him attacked by three men, and as they ran to his assistance the men took flight and escaped in a car that was standing near. David was not much hurt. He soon recovered, and then got a taxi and drove to St. James's. Mr. Ramenez was there, but — '

'Ramenez?' Quest interrupted, with a quick start.

'Yes, Juan Ramenez,' Carol Renoff answered. 'That is the name of David's friend. He was at his chambers, but he was not ill, and he didn't know a thing about the letter. It was a forgery, Mr. Quest. Now you can understand why I am so worried. I do hope you can do something. I am certain that if not David will be murdered. There have been three attempts on his life, and there will be another unless you can prevent it. He is absolutely fearless, or else he won't admit that he is frightened. Anyway, he won't go to the police, and he wouldn't come to you.'

'He was very foolish. He should have gone to the police. By the way, has there been anything in the papers about these alarming incidents?'

'No. As for the last attempt, David told the two constables not to report the affair, and gave them a tip.'

'Why, Miss Renoff?'

'He didn't want any publicity, I suppose.'

The detective's face was grave. He was keenly interested in what he had heard, and particularly so because he suspected that there might be a link between these sinister attempts and the case on which he was working.

'It sounds very mysterious,' said Quest, 'and there must, of course, be a strong motive at the back of it. Has Mr. Morley any idea who these men can be? Or any reason why these attempts on his life should have been made?'

'No, no idea at all. To the best of his knowledge he hasn't an enemy. I have questioned him myself.'

'Do you believe he has told you the truth?'

'I am quite sure he has, Mr. Quest. He would not have told me a lie. He is no wiser than you are. He can't throw any light on the mystery.'

'And you can't, either?'

'No. The only thing that occurred to me, though, was that perhaps they wanted to kidnap him, and make him pay a lot of money to be released.'

Philip Quest did not answer.

'How long has Mr. Morley been acquainted with Juan Ramenez?' he asked after a pause.

'He first met him two or three weeks ago, at a club,' replied Miss Renoff.

'Are the two on intimate terms?'

'Yes, very intimate. Mr. Ramenez is such a charming gentleman that David took a great liking to him. I have met him and I like him, too.'

'Is Mr. Morley familiar with Juan Ramenez's handwriting?'

'Oh, yes. He has had several letters from him.'

'And he was readily deceived by that letter he received the other night?'

'He hadn't a doubt that it was genuine. He told me afterwards that it was a most perfect forgery.'

'How did he account for the use of his friend's name to lure him into a trap, Miss Renoff?'

'He said the letter must have been written by some person who knew he was intimate with Mr. Ramenez.'

Quest put another question.

'Has Mr. Morley any relatives living?' he asked.

'Not one,' the girl answered. 'He is the last of his family.'

'Then in the event of his dying unmarried his estate would go to the Crown?'

'Yes, there is no one to claim it.'

The information Quest had got had strengthened his suspicion. He promised Carol Renoff to take up the matter, and after she was gone he sat and thought over the whole thing, puzzling his brains until nearly twelve o'clock, when Richard Lester came in.

He had nothing much to report. He had shadowed Dr. Burgin from Lime Grove to a West End restaurant, where he had dined with Juan Ramenez, and had subsequently followed him back to his home.

The detective listened to his young partner's statement, and then told him of his interview with the girl, repeating all he had learned from her, and laying stress on the decoy letter.

'I've got a grip of the case now,' he continued. 'We are no longer in the dark. There can be no doubt that David Morley is the next victim for Dr. Burgin's murderous intentions. It's plain. Ramenez's scruples have been overcome. It was at the doctor's instigation, of course, that he got acquainted with young Morley. And as for the letter, that was no forgery. I'm sure that was written by Ramenez, who was not afraid that suspicion would fall on him.'

'There are two things that beat me, though,' said Richard Lester. 'In the first place, since we can account for Dr. Burgin's movements every night, he couldn't have taken any personal part in the attempts against Morley. So who were the three men?'

'Ramenez may have been one of them,' replied Quest. 'And the other I daresay were crooks hired by the doctor.'

'H'm! But in the second place, what is the motive for the plot? What is to be gained by murdering David Morley?'

'That's something I can't find out. I haven't the faintest idea, and from what little I know I can't even make a guess. If what Carol Renoff told me is true — '

He broke off and a gleam came into his eyes. Something had occurred to him, but he made no mention of it to Lester.

'Well, the most important thing to do now is to protect David Morley,' he said. 'I shall call on him tomorrow morning.'

7

An Alarm in the Night

Philip Quest and Richard Lester sat late into the night going over the various points in the mysterious affairs. They were on the point of going to bed when they heard a shout from the street and then a veritable tattoo on the front door. The detective hurried down and he had just unlocked the door when a tall young man pushed passed him into the hall, panting heavily.

'Shut the door! Quickly!' he gasped.

Without asking any questions Quest did this and taking the visitor's arm led him through to the consulting room. Here he was able to take stock of the stranger, and then recognised, in the tall fair young man, David Morley, the fiancé of Carol Renoff, and the object of Dr. Burgin's sinister attentions.

In a few seconds Morley regained his

calm, and there was a sheepish expression on his face, as if he was slightly ashamed of his undignified entrance.

'I don't know what you must think of me, sir,' he said at length, as he dropped into a chair. 'Forgive me for disturbing you at such an hour. But I could do nothing else.'

'But what happened to make you shout in the street?' said Quest. 'Has something else occurred, Mr. Morley?'

David Morley looked up with surprise.

'You know me?' he asked.

'I have seen you quite a lot,' smiled Quest. 'Also Miss Renoff told me of your experiences.'

'She did come to you then,' said Morley. 'I can't blame her. I should have come myself after the second attempt. Did Carol tell you everything?'

'Yes, I had the whole story from her. I know about the three mysterious attempts against you, and I meant to pay you a visit in the morning. In fact it was because my partner and I were discussing your affair that we had stayed up so late. And now tell me, what has happened tonight?

Something must have happened to have brought you here so late, and in such a hurry.'

'Something has,' replied Morley with a grim smile. 'This time it was more serious than any of the others. I dined alone in the West End, Mr. Quest, and then went to a theatre. I got home about twelve o'clock. I didn't feel like going to bed so sat in the library reading until I felt sleepy. I went upstairs to my room intending to go to bed, when I heard a dog barking in the mews at the rear of my house. I don't know what prompted me, but for some reason I went to a dark room at the back of the house and peeped out of the window. To my surprise I saw two men in the garden below, lurking in the shrubbery. Without putting on any lights I went to a window in the front of the house. There I made a startling discovery. Against the park railings, opposite my house, were two other figures, and further up the street I could see the outline of a car.

'Satisfied that it was the intention of the four men to break into the house and kidnap me, I went down to the library to telephone for the police, and found that the instrument would not work. What with the strain I had been under for days and the discoveries I had just made, I must have lost my nerve. For the first time I was really frightened. I felt so utterly helpless. There was only one thought in my mind, and that was to get to you as quickly as possible. I took my overcoat and hat from the hall, slipped down to the basement, opened the door leading to the area, and got out by the servants entrance.

'I couldn't see the two men who had been standing by the park railings, but the car was still there. As soon as I turned the corner of Mount Street I got into a taxi. I knew your address because Carol had been urging me to come to you for days. As far as I knew I was not followed. About two hundred yards from here something went wrong with the engine and I had to get out. I paid the driver, and walked on. Just before I got to your door I saw a closed car coming along behind me, and I lost my nerve again.

That is why I called to you and pounded on the door.

'It's fortunate that you did,' said Philip Quest. 'The noise brought me down in a hurry. You seem to have had a nasty escape.'

'This is the fourth one,' said David Morley. 'They'll probably get me the next time.'

'There won't be a next time, not if I can help it. I wish you had come to me days ago.'

'I wish I had. But I have been in a dogged sort of mood. I was determined to show the scoundrels I hadn't any fear of them.'

'I admire your pluck, but not your discretion,' said the detective wrily. 'Please tell me exactly what has happened, you may be able to give me more information than Miss Renoff did. I gathered from her that you cannot in the least account for these strange occurrences.'

'I can't,' declared David Morley. 'It's an absolute mystery to me. I haven't a relative living, and to the best of my belief

I haven't an enemy in the world.'

'Are you sure you can't think of an explanation?' asked Quest.

'No plausible one. I can only think that the object of the men is to get me in their power and extort money from me.'

'That won't do. It is too weak. No, there is a deeper motive than that. You are a wealthy man, I understand?'

'Fairly so, Mr. Quest. I have an income of forty-thousand pounds a year, inherited from my father.'

'Had he any relative of whom he had lost track?'

'There was no one, I am certain. He had only a brother and he has been dead for some years.'

'The brother died unmarried?'

'Yes, he never married.'

Quest was silent for a moment. He was reluctant, at the present moment, to tell the young man what knowledge he had of the plot against him. Moreover, were he to do so it would probably not lead to any information.

'Miss Renoff gave me full particulars of what has occurred,' he continued. 'She spoke of a friend of yours, Juan Ramenez. You are very intimate with him?'

'We are the best of friends,' David Morley answered. 'He is a Spaniard, and a fine fellow. It was by the use of his name, by a forged letter I believed to have been written by him, that I was lured into a trap. It was a most clever forgery. I could have sworn Ramenez wrote the letter.'

'The forger, whoever he was, must have had a specimen of your friend's handwriting. How could he have obtained it?'

'I can't tell you, Mr. Quest. I asked Ramenez, and he did not know. He was very much puzzled.'

'Has he ever introduced you to a friend of his, a Dr. Francis Burgin, of St. John's Wood?'

'No, I haven't met him.'

'Has Juan Ramenez ever spoken of him?'

'Yes, he said the doctor was a very brilliant man, and he hoped I would meet him some day.'

'Well, it doesn't seem that you can help me very much, Morley. I shall have to rely on my own efforts.'

'You are going to try to find out who my enemies are, sir, and what motive they have?'

'I am. I promised Miss Renoff that I would take the matter up, and I shall.'

During the conversation Quest had been strolling to and fro, passing and repassing the two windows, and throwing his shadow on them.

'The first thing,' he resumed, 'will be to protect you from these determined men. You must keep away from your house in Beverly Street.'

David Morley shook his head.

'I'm not a coward,' he declared. 'I'm not running away!'

'I insist,' said Quest. 'Please be guided by me.'

'I had rather not. I don't like the idea.'

'I don't suppose you do, Morley. But you must get out of London for a time. Stay in the country, or' — as Morley shook his head — 'in the suburbs. I will find you a place, and in the meantime you will be my guest. I'll let your servants know that — '

There was a shattering sound. A pane of glass from one of the windows fell in a shower of splinters to the floor, and at the same instant a bullet hissed by Quest's head and smashed a jar that was on a cabinet behind him.

The detective and Lester stared at each other in amazement. David Morley leaped to his feet.

'They've come back!' he said. 'They shot at your shadow, Mr. Quest!'

A throbbing noise was heard. Quest switched off the light, and moving the blind of the shattered window, peered cautiously out.

'They've gone,' he said. 'I saw the tail light of a car going up the street. It must have come up very quietly and stopped outside the house for a moment.'

He switched on the light and sat down, quite indifferent to what had just happened.

'Things are getting serious, Mr. Quest,' said Lester, as he picked up the pieces of china. 'That's a warning. That shot was for you.'

'Yes, a challenge from Dr. Burgin,'

replied Quest. 'It amounts to that, though I don't think Burgin was in the car.'

David Morley looked at him in surprise.

'Dr. Burgin?' he said in a puzzled tone. 'Juan Ramenez's friend? What do you mean, sir? He isn't one of my enemies, is he?'

'He is, as it happens,' the detective replied. 'I am as puzzled as you are in regard to the motive for the plot against you, but two of the persons concerned in the plot are known to me, and Dr. Burgin is one of them. I will tell you the whole story tomorrow. Well, Mr. Morley, what about the suggestion of going out of town?'

'I think you're right. I'll do whatever you say.'

'Very sensible of you,' said Quest. 'And now you had better go to bed. Lester, take Mr. Morley to the spare room. I'll slip round to Beverly Street. I must see your servants before they discover you are missing. If I wait until the morning they might report your disappearance to the police, and I'd like to prevent that. I must!'

8

The Vanished Watcher

The interval that elapsed between the night of the fourth attempt on David Morley and the point when the tranquil current of events was convulsed by sensational happenings, may be briefly told.

For three days David Morley and Richard Lester had been living in a furnished flat in Regal Mansions, Roehampton Lane, an address that had been withheld, even from Carol Renoff, who merely knew that he had moved from his house to a safe hiding place in the suburbs.

Meanwhile Philip Quest had been shadowing Juan Ramenez, with no results worth mentioning, and a Scotland Yard man, of the name of Dawe, had been guardedly watching Dr. Burgin's residence in Lime Grove, and had learned nothing of any importance. Quest had called on Robert Ferris and told him of the happenings, the morning after David Morley had rushed to him for help, and that official had immediately repeated his offer, that he should loan Quest the use of some of his men.

During those three days, Quest, pursuing his fruitless task, had been aware, without discovering any ocular evidence of it, that he himself was under surveillance, persistently dogged by some person who was too clever to be caught in that act. The detective presumed that this was due to the fact that David Morley's enemies knew of his disappearance, and hoped to find out where he was by keeping an eye on the detective.

It was not a new experience for Quest, and it did not cause him much uneasiness, though the espionage might be a menace to his life. Had he an inkling of what he was to learn in the future, the horror that was at the bottom of these mysteries he was trying to solve, he would probably have known what fear was, with all his intrepid courage.

It was on the night of the third day that things began to move. Having shadowed Juan Ramenez from a West End restaurant to a theatre, Quest left him there and went home at nine o'clock to see if there was a letter or any message from Lester.

He met the maid in the hall, and she looked at him in surprise.

'Do you want dinner, sir? I've just cleared the table. When you rushed out without waiting for it I thought you would have dinner out.'

Quest stared at her blankly.

'What are you talking about?'

'About your dinner, sir. You didn't say you were coming back.'

'Your wits must be wandering. I haven't been home since this morning.'

'You — you what?'

'You heard what I said.'

'But you came in half an hour ago, and went out soon after.'

'I most certainly did not. What do you mean?'

'Then it was your double, sir. I was at the top of the stairs when a gentleman let himself into the house with a key, and went into the consulting room. He looked just like you, and he was dressed the same as you are.'

Quest was amazed.

'How long was he here?'

'Between five and ten minutes, sir,' was the reply.

'Did you see the man again when he left?'

'No, sir, I only heard him go out. I could have sworn — '

Quest did not stop to hear any more. He quickly went through to the consulting room, switched on the light, and glanced around. Everything was in order here.

Then he unlocked his desk and raised the lid, and saw at once that the contents were in some confusion. His letters and papers had been disturbed, but so far as he could tell nothing was missing.

The explanation was obvious. Some clever rogue in Dr. Burgin's pay had impersonated the detective, got into the house with a duplicate key, and opened the desk with another. No doubt his motive had been to learn where David

Morley was living.

He had failed to get the information, however, for Quest had written to Richard Lester that morning and had taken the letter with him and posted it.

'The daring scoundrel!' he said to himself. 'They must have studied my appearance, and knew when I was absent. So this is what Dr. Burgin is capable of. He must have a number of crooked friends in London, who will do anything for money, and are assisting him in his designs on young Morley. They carry out his instructions while he and Ramenez remain in the background.'

There was a knock on the door and the maid entered.

'Mr. Ferris telephoned, sir. I forgot to give you the message when you came in.'

'Robert Ferris, eh? What was the message?'

'I was to tell you he wished to see you most urgently, and he was coming along in a taxi.'

'How long ago did he ring up?'

'Not more than a quarter of an hour before you got home, sir.'

The maid withdrew, and almost immediately a taxi stopped in front of the house. Robert Ferris had arrived. He was admitted and came through to the consulting room.

He was rather pale, and there was a strained, anxious look in his eyes. It was evident that he had brought some bad news.

'What's wrong?' asked Quest.

'Something serious!' cried Robert Ferris. 'Dawe, the man who has been keeping watch on Burgin's house has — '

'Not been murdered?'

'I don't know. He has disappeared under amazing circumstances. It is almost incredible! I had hardly more than left him when — '

Robert Ferris broke off.

'I'll tell you the whole story,' he continued, in an agitated voice. 'A matter of importance cropped up at the Yard this evening in connection with some secret work Dawe did for my branch a couple of weeks ago. It was necessary that I should get information from him, so I took a taxi to St. John's Wood. I got out before it reached Burgin's house, and walked down. Dawe was standing on the pavement by the garden wall, in the shadows of some overhanging trees, and about three yards from the gateway. There was nothing to report. Neither the doctor nor the servant had been out of the house during the day. After he had given me the information I wanted I left him, and I had gone a short distance down the road, not more than a hundred yards, when I remembered something that I had forgotten to ask him. I walked quickly back, and to my amazement — '

Ferris paused again.

'Dawe had disappeared,' he went on. 'There was no sign of him, but his cap was there on the pavement, and a cigarette he had been smoking while I talked to him was lying near, still burning. There was no sign of a struggle. I crept to the gateway, and peered into the garden, listening, and I distinctly heard a door click shut. I felt sure that Dawe had fallen into the hands of Dr. Burgin, and my first impulse was to force an entry into the house. On second thoughts I realised that would be madness, might have cost me my life, too, so — '

'One moment,' interrupted Quest. 'Was the gate locked?'

'No,' replied Robert Ferris.

'What do you suppose happened to Dawe?'

'I should say that he was struck down from above, from the top of the garden wall, while he was standing there in the shadow, and shortly after I left him. The blow was dealt by either Dr. Burgin or his servant, and the two of them hurried out, picked him up and carried him into the house.'

'It seems likely. The doctor must have suspected that Dawe was a police spy, and has been waiting for a chance to get at him. The daring of it is staggering, Ferris. There is no limit to that scoundrel's audacity. Go on. What did you do?'

'A constable came along, so I left him to keep watch, hurried to the local police station, and had them send three men to Lime Grove, with instructions to stay there until I joined them. Then I got a taxi to Scotland Yard and had a search warrant made out.'

'That's good,' said Quest. 'You're sure Dawe is in the doctor's house?'

'I'm sure of it — dead or alive.'

'I'm glad you called for me. We'll go over there immediately. This is where we have the doctor in a trap.'

'I think so, too. If he has murdered Dawe he won't be able to move the body with the police watching the house.'

'No, it would be impossible. There is only the one way out. The garden, I remember, is shut in on both sides, and at the rear by the gardens of other residences.'

They set off immediately, picked up a taxi at the end of the road, and in twenty minutes were at the bottom of Lime Grove. Here they left the cab and walked on to Number 6, where the four constables were in the shadows of the garden wall. Their report was satisfactory. Since they had been on duty nobody had come out to the street, and they had not seen or heard anything from within.

At Robert Ferris' instructions they

followed him and the detective into the garden, up the path, and waited with him by the door.

Oscar Prantz answered the summons, and before he could utter a word the whole party had brushed by him into the hall.

Dr. Burgin appeared from the library, wearing a smoking jacket of black velvet and a skull cap of the same material. He was perfectly cool, but there was a gleam of anger in his eyes.

'Ah, Mr. Ferris and Mr. Quest again,' he said blandly. 'And the police! What right have you to force yourselves in here? I must insist on your departing at once.'

Quest shook his head.

'I don't think so,' he said. 'We have a search warrant.'

The doctor smiled.

'Indeed!' he murmured. 'If that is the case you are at liberty to search where you like. I am at a loss to understand, though, what you expect to find.'

'I don't think you are, sir. We have come to look for a Scotland Yard detective who mysteriously vanished tonight while he was standing in the shadow of your garden wall.'

'May I ask what he was doing there, Mr. Quest?'

'He was acting under orders. That is all I have to tell you.'

'And you are inclined to connect me with his disappearance? You suspect that I have knowledge of his whereabouts?'

'We are quite sure you have. We have every reason to believe that the man is in the house, alive or dead.'

'Absurd! This is really too much. My patience is exhausted! I consider it an outrage that you should insult me like this, and I strongly resent it. I shall complain to Scotland Yard of your conduct. I have no knowledge whatever of the man you are looking for, and I can't imagine why — '

'That's a lie!' broke in Robert Ferris, losing his temper. 'You and your rascally servant have got him in here somewhere. You've probably murdered him!'

Doctor Burgin's face did not show the least sign of fear at this accusation. There was a glimmer of amusement in his eyes.

He was silent for a moment, and then he shrugged his shoulders and laughed softly.

'What nonsense!' he said. 'This is really ridiculous! It is beneath my dignity to take you seriously! This is the third visit you have paid me, for no sound reason, and I trust it will be the last! It is fortunate for you that I have a sense of humour. Even if you had no warrant I should insist on your making a search. Please get on with it, and then leave me in peace. I will help you all I can, as I did on the previous occasions when you annoyed me by your stupid suspicions.'

The doctor's words sounded sincere. Was he indifferent to a search? Or was he concealing, by an air of bluff, his dread of what they might find?

Quest looked at Robert Ferris significantly. There was a misgiving in his mind. In spite of his absolute conviction that Dr. Burgin had in some way got hold of the Scotland Yard man, he was afraid that in some unaccountable way he had contrived to cover up the crime.

And so it was proved. Two of the

113

constables went out into the garden, taking Oscar Prantz with them, and Quest and Ferris and the other two constables scoured the whole house, accompanied by the doctor.

They ransacked it from top to bottom, tapping walls, as before, sounding the floors, and looking into every cupboard and chest.

But they were completely baffled. They found nothing which could even remotely suggest that Dawe had been on the premises.

And it was the same with those who searched the garden. They were no more successful. When they came into the house they stated that there were no footprints, no trace of anybody, and no spot where the earth had been disturbed.

During the search the doctor had been suave, polite, bland in his manner, going from floor to floor without hesitation, with an air of perfect confidence.

If Dawe had been murdered what had happened to the corpse? And if not, what was the explanation of his disappearance?

He could not have been carried off in a taxi or a private car. Robert Ferris was positive that no vehicle of any kind had passed along Lime Grove between the time he had left Dawe and the time he had got back to find him missing — an interval of five minutes at the most.

At the finish of the search the constables were dismissed, with instructions not to speak of the search or of the missing Dawe, and Dr. Burgin took Quest and Ferris into the library. His manner was still courteous, though a trifle stiff.

'I hope you are satisfied now, gentlemen,' he said, 'that there was not the slightest ground for your suspicions. You have caused me a great deal of pain and humiliation. I am not resentful, however. I realise that you only did your duty. To show that there is no ill feeling on my part, will you let me offer you a cigar and a drink.'

While he was speaking he had stepped to a large and heavy cabinet, and unlocked and opened the double doors. There were three deep shelves within. On the two lower ones were a number of decanters filled with spirits and some boxes of cigars. On the top shelf, heaped together in confusion, was what appeared to be a collection of old manuscripts.

Quest and Robert Ferris declined to have either a drink or a cigar. The doctor replaced the box of cigars he had taken out, and as he did so he must have dislodged one of the manuscripts.

He tried to catch it, but missed, and it fell to the floor within reach of Quest, who picked it up. He glanced at it, and his interest was stirred.

He had in his hand a parchment that was yellow with age. The cover had illuminated borders, and an inscription, neatly penned in Italian, stated that the contents of the folio was a history of the Black Arts.

For a fraction of a second Dr. Burgin's eyes betrayed just a glimmer of uneasiness, but the next instant he was his bland self again, his features as emotionless as a mask.

'Collecting ancient manuscripts is a hobby of mine, Mr. Quest,' he remarked, as he took the folio from him.

'And to study them?' The detective quietly asked.

'Of course,' the doctor assented. 'I am familiar with most of the European languages.'

'You have some knowledge of the Black Arts, perhaps?'

'Little or none, Mr. Quest. Their secret perished with them, and it is as well they did.'

'I agree with you, doctor. If I remember rightly, in the days when the Black Arts flourished murder was much easier and safer than it is in the present day. Detection was almost impossible.'

Dr. Burgin nodded.

'That is quite true, I believe,' he replied, looking straight at Quest. 'Murder could be committed with impunity. It is different in our time, with modern science to combat the ingenuity of the criminal.'

'I am not so sure. There have been instances which prove the contrary.'

'There always will be, sir. They are very rare, though. But we were talking of the manuscript you have just seen. It is

117

hundreds of years old, and the only one of its kind in existence. I discovered it several years ago while I was delving amongst the literary treasures of an ancient monastery near the Italian town of Sienna. With much difficulty I persuaded the monks to sell it to me, at an exorbitant price.'

'I am interested in such manuscripts, doctor. Would you allow me to take this home and read it at my leisure?'

'I am sorry to refuse, Mr. Quest. I prize the folio so highly that I could not let it pass out of my hands. If you were to read it here — '

'I think not. No, thank you.'

Dr. Burgin put the manuscript back on the shelf, and with a curt farewell Quest and Robert Ferris departed. Oscar Prantz opened the front door for them.

They were glad to be away from the presence of the man whose specious lies, mocking courtesy and blandness, provoked them almost beyond endurance.

They discussed the failure of their search as they left Lime Grove. They were utterly mystified. That Dawe had been murdered by Dr. Burgin there was no doubt, but what had become of the body? By what means had the doctor disposed of it?

'We'll never know, I'm afraid,' said Robert Ferris. 'The fate of Dawe will remain as deep a mystery as the disappearance of Renault. I'm certain they were both murdered in that house.'

He continued to talk of the mystery, but got no answers to his remarks. Philip Quest walked by his side in silence, his mind absorbed in something else. He was thinking of the parchment folio that dealt with the Black Arts. Could that, he wondered, hold the key to the inexplicable disappearance of the watcher from Scotland Yard?

9

A Discovery

It was on Tuesday night that George Dawe vanished so mysteriously from Lime Grove, and on the following Thursday there was another daring move in the contest of craft and wits between Philip Quest and Dr. Francis Burgin.

It was late in the afternoon. David Morley and Richard Lester had been for a walk and had returned to the flat in Regal Mansions. It was on the first floor, in the front of the house, and it belonged, as the present occupants knew, to a gentleman of the name of Wright, who had let it for a short period before going abroad.

Morley was reading on a couch in the sitting room, and Lester was standing by the window, gazing over at the wide stretch of the Polo Ground. They knew of the events of the Tuesday. Quest had informed them by letter, and they were hoping soon to have further and better news from him.

Lester noticed a small furniture van, with no name on it, that was coming along Roehampton Lane. It stopped in front of Regal Mansions. Three burly men descended from it, and opened the door at the back, lifted out a large, antique chest of carved oak, and carried it into the building.

He turned away from the window and sat down. Shortly afterwards he heard shuffling sounds on the stairs and in the hall, and then a rap at the door. He opened it and saw the three men with their burden.

'Are you Mr. Wright?' one of them asked.

'No,' answered Lester. 'Mr. Wright is not here now. He has gone abroad for a time.'

'Well, this chest is for him,' said the man. 'He bought it a couple of weeks ago from Mr. Rothstein, the antique dealer of Wardour Street. It was to be sent to this address as soon as it was restored.'

'I don't know anything about that. You had better take the chest away and bring it back when Mr. Wright has returned.'

'Take it away? No, sir, our orders were to leave it here.'

'Is there anything to pay on it?'

'No, there's nothing to collect.'

'You'd better bring it in then. I suppose it's all right.'

The men carried the chest into the room and placed it on the floor. The man who had done the talking pushed the door shut and handed the young man a piece of paper.

'Will you sign this, please,' he said. 'Mr. Rothstein wants a receipt, and as — '

Whipping a short, thick stick from his pocket as he spoke he sprang at Lester and struck him on the head. It was a stunning blow, and as he reeled to the floor, his senses swimming, he dimly saw all three of the men hurl themselves at David Morley, and heard him give a startled cry. Of what followed he had no recollection.

★　★　★

When Lester returned to consciousness, with an aching head, he was alone in the room, bound and gagged on the couch. The antique chest had disappeared. The men were gone, and so was David Morley.

The truth flashed quickly to his mind. The three men were in the pay of Dr. Burgin, and they had learned by enquiries that the flat had formerly been occupied by Mr. Wright.

Equipped with that information, to lend colour to the tale they meant to tell, they had come here today, got access by a ruse, and carried David Morley off in the chest, which they had brought for that purpose.

But how could they have discovered that he was hiding at the Regal Mansions? Lester did not give too much time to that problem. He was nearly frantic.

His sole idea was to get out of his bonds and try and find out what had happened to his charge.

For a little while he tugged and strained at the cords that bound him, but it was no use, they had been tied too tightly to be eased in any way.

He was just about to give up, exhausted by his efforts, when he heard footsteps and the rattle of crockery in the passage, and remembered that it was about time for Jones, the service-porter of the building to bring tea.

The man stopped and tried the door. It was locked, and presumably the key had been removed. The porter rapped twice, then moved away. In the hope of alarming him Lester threw himself from the couch to the floor.

The footsteps returned. Jones had heard the dull thud. He called again, and again, and then knowing that something must be wrong, unlocked the door with his own key. When he saw what had happened he hurried in, banged the tray down on the table, and hastened over to the helpless man.

'Good Heavens!' he cried. 'What's happened?'

He tore off the handkerchief that was tied across Lester's mouth, and cut his wrists and ankles free with a knife. He stumbled to his feet, little the worse for the blow that had stunned him.

'Have you had burglars, sir?'

'Worse than that. The three men who brought the chest have kidnapped Mr. Morley.'

'Kidnapped him? Oh, no, sir. I saw them leave, and Mr. Morley wasn't with them. I watched them lift the chest into the van and — '

'Mr. Morley was inside the chest.'

'Inside? But — What — ' The porter's eyes opened wide and his mouth dropped.

'Never mind, Jones. I haven't time to explain! How long have the men been gone?'

'Not more than a quarter of an hour, sir.'

'Did you see them leave?'

'Yes, sir, I watched them out of the Lane. They turned in the direction of Hammersmith Bridge.'

A start of only a quarter of an hour. It was better than he had expected. He thought he had been unconscious for longer than that.

He snatched his hat, and having told

the bewildered porter not to speak to anyone of what had happened, flew downstairs and out of the building, and ran fast down Roehampton Lane. There might be a chance of overtaking the men, he felt, for he supposed they were going to St. John's Wood.

Near Hammersmith Bridge he hailed a taxi and told the driver to make for the Fulham Road. When they had gone for a short distance he told the driver to stop when he saw a policeman. A little further on there was one. The driver stopped and Lester leaned out of the window and questioned him.

'I'm looking for a small furniture van, no name on it, with three big fellows riding. Have you seen anything of it?'

'I'm not sure,' said the constable slowly, so slowly that Lester began to fume. 'Let me think. Furniture van. No name. Three men. Yes, sir. Now I come to think of it there was a small van. I remember it had to stop at this corner, a man with a fruit barrow was crossing and held up the road. It turned down towards the King's Road.'

'How long ago?'

'Not more than ten minutes,' was the reply.

Lester thanked him and told the driver to take the King's Road. He was getting more confident of success as he drove on. Luck was with him. That hold-up put the van back a minute or so and there was a chance that they might come along with them in the King's Road. Lester wished with all his might that traffic lights and policemen would go against the van. It was his only chance. Failing that he would go straight to St. John's Wood and watch Dr. Burgin's house.

It was growing dark now. The street lamps were flashing in the dusk of the evening. They held to the King's Road, and he watched all the vehicles ahead of him. At length, when he was within a short stretch of Sloane Square, his heart gave a quick jump.

'There it is!' he said to himself.

He stopped the cab, got out and paid the driver, and then hurried forward for a few yards to a van that was standing by the kerb. It was the van he was looking for. The doors at the back were open, the antique chest was inside, but there was no sign of the men.

A small crowd had gathered at the spot and Lester looked quickly round them to see if the men had only got down. But there was no one amongst the crowd who so much as resembled any of the burly men who had brought the chest to the flat.

He pushed his way in and spoke to the constable, who was writing in his notebook.

'What is wrong here?' he enquired.

'Can't say, sir. This van has been abandoned, and there is nothing to show where it belongs.'

'There were three men in it,' said Lester. 'What has become of them?'

'I don't know,' replied the constable. 'They were seen to jump down and take to their heels. That's all any of these people can tell me.'

'Well, I can tell you something. There is a man inside that chest. He might even be murdered.'

'What? A dead man inside?'

'I shouldn't be surprised if he has been murdered,' said Lester. 'He was kidnapped from a flat in Roehampton Lane and carried off in this van. I've been chasing it with a taxi.'

There was a gasp from the spectators. Willing hands helped the constable lift the chest from the van, and when it was on the pavement the lid was lifted. For a second or two there was silence. Then the crowd began to laugh and jeer.

The chest was empty!

Lester stared at it in blank stupefaction, scarcely able to believe his eyes.

'I've — there's some mistake,' he stammered. 'I was sure — '

'Is this your idea of a joke!' snapped the constable angrily. 'Murdered man! Kidnapping! I think you'd better come along and explain to the station sergeant!'

Those people on the outskirts of the crowd were pressing forward, eager to get a close look at the chest. The constable was jostled roughly against the chest, and Lester, who had good reason for not wanting to 'explain' to the station sergeant, seized his opportunity and slipped through the crowd into the open road.

Nobody noticed him go, for which he was thankful. He made his way back to the flat torn between hope and apprehension.

It was certain that David Morley had been removed from the flat in the chest. There was no question about it. Had his dead body been left somewhere? No, not in a crowded street. That was impossible.

The only plausible explanation was that he had managed to escape from the chest, and had dropped out of the van, and that the three men, having discovered that he was missing, had abandoned the van, and fled from fear of arrest.

Lester was certain that that was what had happened. It was foolish to worry. Morley would turn up all right. So he believed. But a disappointment awaited him when he arrived at Regal Mansions. David Morley was not in the flat. He had not come back, and Jones had had no message from him.

What had happened? Where could he be?

His fears were revived. He stayed at the flat for an hour in the hope of something — some message from Morley. But there was nothing.

The next and important thing was to get to Philip Quest. On his way out he went into the porter's office and with a small bribe extracted from that very curious man a promise not to mention the affair of the afternoon.

Arriving at the City he was relieved to find that Quest was at home, but David Morley was not there.

He told the detective what had happened, and he was greatly upset when he heard the story. The audacity of the trick amazed him. He was inclined to agree with Lester's idea that Morley was alive, and had escaped from the oak chest.

'But what has become of him? I should have thought he would have gone back to the flat. He must have known how worried you would be. Or he might have come to me.'

'Perhaps he was afraid to,' suggested Lester.

'He wouldn't have been afraid to come to me,' said Quest.

'Probably he has gone to his house in Beverly Street.'

'No, I don't think he'd go there. I don't know what to think. This is worrying me.'

'I'm worried, too. It looks as if something has happened to the fellow after he escaped By the way, how could Dr. Burgin have learned that David Morley and I were living at the Regal Mansions? That's what puzzles me.'

'I can't account for that, not in the least. I thought it would have been impossible for — '

Quest broke off abruptly. Something had occurred to him. He rose, and going to his desk, picked up the blotting-pad and showed it to his partner.

'This is how they found out,' he said. 'I wrote a letter to you and posted it on Tuesday morning, the day that cunning rogue got into the place by impersonating me, and ransacked my desk. I remember pressing the envelope to the pad, I was in a hurry and didn't wait for it to dry, and the man must have examined it. Probably held it to the mirror and was thus able to read the address.'

'That might explain it,' said Lester dubiously, 'but the address isn't readable now.'

'No, you couldn't read anything on it now,' Quest replied. 'But that blotting paper was clean on Tuesday, I remember changing it before I started my letters. I only had a few to answer on Tuesday, but I've used it a lot since.'

'Well, that's cleared up that point. Pity you didn't think of that before.'

'Yes, a great pity, but it's no use grumbling, the damage is done.'

They waited for some time, hoping that Morley would come and while they waited they discussed Dr. Burgin and the mysterious disappearance of Dawe, and Quest told his young partner of the ancient manuscript dealing with the Black Arts.

At supper time they decided that it was no use waiting for Morley, something must be done, and after they had eaten Quest decided that Lester should stay at home while he went out to make some enquiries.

He was gone for more than an hour, and when he returned his face was grave. He had no good news. He was troubled as he dropped into a chair.

'I have been to the flat,' he said, 'and also to Morley's house in Beverly Street. He has not been to the flat and not sent any message, and nothing has been heard of him at his house.'

'That's bad,' answered Lester. 'Something certainly has happened to him.'

'I think so. How else are we to account for — '

As Quest spoke there was a tap at the door, and the maid came in, a letter in her hand.

'This has just come by special messenger,' she said.

She left the room, and Quest tore the letter open. His face brightened as he glanced at it.

'It's from Morley,' he said, and began to read it aloud.

'478, Cresswell Road.
'Thursday night.
'DEAR MR. QUEST,

'If you have learned what happened this afternoon you must be very worried about me. I dare say you do know, for I don't think Lester was badly hurt. He probably soon recovered, and if not he would have been found by the porter when he came with the tea. I will tell you what happened briefly.

'Three men arrived in a furniture van, and came upstairs with an antique chest which they claimed had been bought in Wardour Street by the former occupant of the flat, Mr. Wright. By that ruse they got into our sitting room, and they had hardly more than put the chest down when they attacked us. One of the men struck Lester on the head with a piece of wood, knocking him down, and the next instant all three of them threw themselves on me.

'I was drugged almost before I could open my lips. The next thing I knew I was in the chest, which was obviously

135

in the van, for I could feel the jolting of it and the noise of the engine. My wrists were tied and I was gagged with a handkerchief. I felt rotten, but after much trouble I managed to get my hands free and tore off the gag. I raised the lid of the chest. The three men must have been in the front for there was nobody in the van. I got out of the chest, pushed open the doors, and when the van had to slow down I jumped out.

'It was dark at the time, and I discovered that I was in the King's Road, Chelsea. I don't remember very much else for a time, my mind must have been heavy with the drug, I suppose. I think I wandered for some time, for when I began to remember clearly I was in a public house at Earl's Court, drinking brandy. I felt much better after that.

'I couldn't decide what to do. I dared not go back to the flat or to my house, and I was scared of coming across London to you. I was afraid there might be a watch on each of the places.

Suddenly it occurred to me to go to Mr. Renoff's house in Cresswell Road. I did so, and I need hardly tell you how glad they were to see me. Though they were thankful that you were looking after me, the absence of any knowledge of what was happening had worried them greatly.

'I intended to telephone you, but soon after I arrived I had another spell when my mind was almost a blank. It must have been a queer sort of drug I was knocked out with, to have such recurrent effects.

'I shall stay where I am for the present. I think it will be safer, but I will be guided by you. Perhaps you will come over to Cresswell Road tomorrow to see me. I have been thinking of that amazing story you told me, and I am feeling very depressed. I am tired of being hunted and harried like a criminal. Will I be safe anywhere? Will the mystery ever be cleared up? Why is Dr. Burgin so determined to get me in his power, and why is Juan Ramenez, the man I believed to be my friend, helping him to carry out his designs? What is to be gained? It not only baffles me, it worries me. I'm losing my nerve.

'Miss Renoff sends her regards and her gratitude for your efforts on my behalf.

'Please try and get in touch with me tomorrow.

'Yours sincerely,
'DAVID MORLEY.'

Quest looked for a long time at the two closely written pages, half folded it, apparently changed his mind, and then began slowly to tear it in tiny little pieces. Then he went over to the fireplace and dropped the fragments into the glowing coals.

'That's the best thing to do with that,' he remarked. 'I can't be too careful. The man who got into the house on Tuesday may try to get in again.'

Lester nodded.

'There's no telling what will happen,' he said. 'We are up against the most dangerous men I've ever heard of. They get their orders from Dr. Burgin, and he will stick at nothing. Thank goodness they didn't get David Morley. I've had some bad moments about that affair. I might have guessed there was something wrong — '

'Don't be ridiculous!' said Quest sharply. 'How on earth were you to know who they were. I should have acted in the same way had I been in your place. You weren't careless, it's just that they were damn clever. Don't think about it. They didn't get him.'

'What are you going to do?' asked Lester, feeling a little brighter now that Morley was safe and the detectives did not blame him. 'Are you going to let him stay where he is?'

'Only for tonight. It would not be safe.'

'Not safe. Why?'

'For an obvious reason. Ramenez has met Carol Renoff, and knows, of course, that Morley is engaged to her.'

'Yes, I didn't think of that. You will have to find another hiding place for him.'

'There's no immediate hurry. He will be safe there for the present, I hope. His enemies, instructed by Dr. Burgin, will doubtless keep an eye on the flat in Regal Mansions, the house in Beverly Street, and on us. And not until they are satisfied that their man is not at one of the places will it occur to the doctor, or to Juan Ramenez, to have a watch set on Mr. Renoff's residence.'

'I wouldn't count on it, Mr. Quest.'

'No, I know I can't be too sure. That's only my way of working it out. I had better see Morley in the morning and decide where to take him.'

He paused and looked at the clock.

'It's not very late, I know, but I'm going to bed. And you had better go, too. We know that Morley is safe for tonight, and you've had a full day, so an early night won't do you any harm. For myself, I think that we've got some very full days in front of us and maybe some long nights, and the idea of a good night's rest rather appeals to me.'

10

Quest Plays A Dangerous Game

Not for a considerable time, however, was Philip Quest to see his bed. He threw the cigarette-end into the fireplace and rose from his chair. His hand was on the light switch when the telephone bell rang.

He went back and picked up the receiver.

'Hello!' he called.

'Hello!' was the reply. 'Is that Mr. Quest?'

'Yes, speaking.'

'This is David Morley. Did you get my letter?'

'Yes, it arrived a little while ago. I was so glad to hear from you. We have been very worried. How are you?'

'Not too bad. How is Lester?'

'He's all right. He was not hurt much, just stunned.'

'I'm glad of that. I rang you up, Mr.

Quest, because I have just remembered something I forgot to put in the letter — something I thought you ought to know at once. When I opened the chest and climbed out I heard the men speaking, there was a little grill behind the driver's head and I could hear distinctly. One of the men mentioned the name of Ferris and also said something about tonight.'

Quest gave a quick start.

'Are you sure that was the name you heard?'

'Quite sure,' answered Morley. 'I should not have remembered afterwards, perhaps, had I not supposed the man referred to was the Scotland Yard friend you have spoken of.'

'You heard nothing else?'

'No, only what I have told you. Does it mean anything? Do you think there is any reason to be alarmed — '

'I'm afraid there is, Morley. If that's all I'll ring off now. I will call to see you tomorrow. In the meantime, don't go out. Good-bye!'

Quest rang off, and, turning to Lester,

who had waited at the door, hurriedly repeated to him what he had just learned from Morley.

'I am alarmed,' he continued. 'Though the watch on Dr. Burgin has been relaxed since the disappearance of Dawe, Robert Ferris himself has frequently been keeping watch in Lime Grove. It seems, from what Morley overheard while he was in the van, that the doctor has discovered that Ferris was lurking round the place, and has determined to get rid of him, with the aid of the men who played that trick on you at the flat today.'

'You think there is a plot to murder Ferris tonight?' asked Lester.

'It looks very much like it,' said the detective.

'What are we going to do about it? Go to St. John's Wood?'

'No, to Scotland Yard first. Robert Ferris might be there. I should hardly think he would be watching in Lime Grove at this hour. Get your clothes, there's no time to waste.'

Lester hurried out of the room, returning in a few seconds with his hat and coat, and Philip Quest's clothes on his arm.

'I'm so glad we're going to have a good night's rest,' he grinned, as he helped the detective into his coat, and then took from Quest the automatic that he held out to him.

A taxi from Holborn soon took them to the Embankment, and it had no sooner stopped outside the big building, when one of Robert Ferris' staff, James Laring, crossed the pavement and nodded to Quest.

'Mr. Ferris has been and gone, sir,' he said. 'He returned shortly after you left.'

Philip Quest stared at him.

'After I left?' he said. 'What do you mean?'

James Laring seemed surprised.

'You called an hour ago, sir,' he said.

'You've made a mistake. I haven't been in since yesterday.'

'I — I can't be mistaken! It was certainly you, Mr. Quest! I spoke to you and — '

'You didn't speak to me, Laring. I know what happened. It was a trick. The

144

man was my double. A very clever impostor.'

'An impostor? I could have sworn it was you! What was the reason — '

'Never mind that now,' interrupted Quest. 'Tell me what happened.'

'I had just come out to buy some cigarettes when a taxi stopped,' said James Laring, 'and the man who was your double called to me, used my name. He was in a hurry, he said, and would I ask Mr. Ferris to come down and speak to him for a moment. I told him Mr. Ferris was not in, and he said he would call again in the morning, and drove off. I got my cigarettes and went up to my room. During my absence Mr. Ferris had returned. I gave him the message I believed to have come from you, and soon afterwards he left.'

'Were there any other persons in the cab?' asked Quest.

'I couldn't see, sir. It was pretty dark inside.'

'Did the man get out, Laring?'

'No, he lowered the window to speak to me.'

'What have been Mr. Ferris' movements today?' Quest continued.

'He has been doing some special work in the East End, he went out with one of the 'Q' cars,' James Laring replied.

'And where has he gone now? Home?'

'No, sir, to Lime Grove.'

'At this hour of the night? Was it for any particular reason?'

'I don't think so, sir. He told me as he was leaving that perhaps he would learn something if he watched Dr. Burgin's house at a later hour than he did last night.'

'How long will you be at your office, Laring?'

'For some hours, sir. I've got heaps of work to do, and I'm expecting some special information through tonight from abroad.'

'Very well. Be in readiness for a message from me. I am going to St. John's Wood myself, and I shall very possibly want you and a couple of your men to join me there.'

Quest and Lester had remained in the taxi. The driver was told where to take them, and they set off, thinking with anxiety of the startling thing that had occurred.

Quest was right in surmising that there was a plot to murder his friend. The man who had so cleverly impersonated him before had done so again, and at the instignation of Dr. Burgin. At Quest's double he had come boldly to Scotland Yard, and no doubt with two or more companions who had been invisible to James Laring in the darkness of the cab.

It had been a close shave for Robert Ferris. Had he been in his room at the time he would have received the message and come down without suspicion, with the result that he would have been enticed into the cab, and then stunned or drugged.

The cunning plot had failed, but something might have happened to him since. Had his enemies watched for him in Lime Grove, and trapped him there? Had he already vanished off the face of the earth as mysteriously as Pierre Renault and George Dawe?

'If you are so worried, why didn't you

bring Mr. Laring with us instead of telling him to wait for a message from you?'

'Because I didn't think it would be necessary,' Quest replied. 'Though there is every reason to be apprehensive, the chances are that we shall find Robert Ferris safe and sound. For one thing Dr. Burgin is not likely to be keeping any watch at this time of the night. And in the second place I don't believe my double and his companions went from Scotland Yard to St. John's Wood. They very probably decided to abandon their designs for the present.'

Philip Quest's hopes were not realised, however. He and Lester left the taxi at the top of Lime Grove and walked the short distance to Dr. Burgin's residence.

They found the gate locked, and the house in darkness, but they did not see anything of Robert Ferris. They searched for him in vain, strolling the length of the street on one side and then on the other. Then they made a complete circuit of the block, and by the time they came back to Lime Grove and stopped outside Number 6, they felt a chilling sense of horror.

'It looks as if the worst had happened,' said Quest in a gloomy voice.

'I'm afraid so,' assented Lester. 'Mr. Ferris meant to watch here tonight, and no doubt he did.'

'I'm certain of it from what he told Laring. He would tell him exactly where he was going in case he should be needed.'

'Do you think he might have been here and then gone home?'

'It is most improbable. It is not much more than an hour since he left Scotland Yard to come here, and we arrived. If he had been watching he wouldn't have given up so soon, of that I'm sure. No, Lester, Dr. Burgin must have known he was here and has got hold of him. He's in that house, dead or alive!'

'Well, what are we going to do? We can't let the matter rest there. Shall we fetch the police and insist on making a search?'

The detective shook his head.

'That would be useless,' he replied. 'If Ferris has met with the same fate as Dawe and Renault — and it seems very

149

likely — Burgin, by some mysterious means, will hide all traces of his crime. Though how he does it I can't think.'

'So you won't bring the police?'

'I don't think so. It's hardly possible that I have jumped to a wrong conclusion. But perhaps Robert Ferris did change his mind. He might not have come here after all, or he might have kept watch for a while and then gone home. We can do nothing more here. I think the best thing to do would be to go to his house — '

Quest paused, hearing footsteps. He saw a constable approaching, and instantly he walked towards him, telling Lester to follow. The constable peered at them closely and suspiciously as they drew near.

As they met the constable recognised Quest, he had been one of the men sent from the local station on the night of Dawe's disappearance and the search of Burgin's house.

'Good evening, Mr. Quest,' he murmured, touching his helmet.

Quest remembered the man.

'How long have you been on duty in this neighbourhood tonight?' he asked.

'I've been on just two hours, sir,' he said.

'Then perhaps you can help me,' said the detective. 'Did you notice a man lurking near Number 6, the house we went to the other night?'

'Yes, sir. There was a man standing by the wall near the gate, just in the shadow of the tree. I went up to him and spoke to him. He turned out to be Mr. Ferris, of the Yard. I remembered him.'

'Did he have anything to say to you?'

'Very little, sir. He told me he was doing special work, but didn't say what it was.'

'Did you see Mr. Ferris again after you left him?' asked Quest.

'No, sir, I didn't,' the constable replied. 'I looked back when I got to the corner, but I couldn't see him. I was puzzled for a moment. He couldn't have gone away, I knew, for he couldn't have got out of sight in that short time.'

'Then what do you think became of him?'

'He must have slipped into the garden. That's the only thing he could have done.'

'How long ago was this?'

'About half an hour, no more than that.'

'Did you hear any noise behind you while you were walking to the corner?'

'No, Mr. Quest, not even a footstep.'

'Thank you. That's all.'

The constable was curious. He would have liked to have known more. Although Quest had virtually dismissed him he shuffled for a moment before moving on, hoping that the detective might be induced to say more. But as nothing came he touched his helmet and with a muttered 'good night, sir' started again on his beat, leaving them with their worst fears confirmed.

Robert Ferris had not gone home. Without a doubt he had fallen into the clutches of Francis Burgin. What had been his fate? Would any trace of him ever be discovered, or would it be a third case of a complete disappearance.

Quest was sick with horror. Plain

murder he could cope with. In his long career he had had some strange cases to deal with, but never had he come in contact with anything like this. During the weeks he had been working on the case he had not got any further than when he started. All he knew was that Dr. Burgin was the prime mover behind everything that had happened. The reason for the body-snatching, and the complete disappearance of Renault and Dawe, also the four attempts on David Morley's life was unknown to him. The theory that he had formed was so horrible that he scarcely liked to think about it.

'I wonder how it was done,' he said to Lester, and his voice shook. 'Was Ferris stunned by a blow dealt from the top of the wall by the doctor or his servant while he was standing there? And carried inside afterwards, when the constable had turned the corner? I think it most likely that he went into the garden, knowing the gate was not locked, and was caught there. Whichever way it was, they have got him.'

'And killed him, I suppose,' replied

Lester. 'Well, now we will have to fetch the police. There is nothing else for it.'

'Yes, there is,' Quest declared. 'It would be useless to fetch the police, we should find nothing. But I'll tell you what I'm going to do. I'm going into that house. I may be able to find out something that will justify the arrest of Dr. Burgin, and lead to his conviction.'

'You mean to break in?'

'I certainly do. I believe I can.'

'Don't be mad! You know what happened to the others. You'll never come out again.'

'Perhaps I shan't. But I'm going to chance it.'

'If it is necessary that somebody should get in let me go,' said Lester. 'If anything should happen to you — '

He broke off. The thought was too horrible. Of all people, Philip Quest was the last person to be allowed to take that chance. Besides which, the bond between these two was more than that of just partnership. Lester was very fond of the clever detective, who had been brother as well as co-partner.

'No, it's too dangerous for you. Anyway, I need somebody reliable to stand by to help in case of emergency. I'd rather know you were outside waiting to help me, than inside and in danger.'

Richard Lester knew it was useless to argue. He gave in with a grunt.

'Very well, have it your own way. How are you going to do it? The gate is locked, and we can't break it open without making a noise.'

'It won't be necessary to break it open. I have something else in mind — a safer plan.'

Quest reflected for a moment. It had suddenly occurred to him that Robert Ferris might be prowling about inside the grounds. But on second thoughts he concluded that this was impossible. He argued that as the gate must have been unlocked when Ferris went into the garden, it would not have been subsequently locked unless he had been caught by Burgin or his servant.

'Come along,' he said to Lester. 'I'll show you what we are going to do. I took a survey of the neighbourhood several days ago, thinking the information might be useful some time.'

Taking pains to elude observation, they went round to a street that ran parallel with Lime Grove, and slipped into a narrow alley which brought them to a wall that was five or six feet in height.

Quest climbed over it without any difficulty, and Lester followed him. They were now in the back garden of a residence that was at the rear of Dr. Burgin's house.

Quietly, and in the shadows, they glided across it to another wall, and mounted to the top of it, and when they had listened for a few seconds, and heard nothing, they cautiously lowered themselves into the doctor's garden.

The house was a short distance beyond them, and they could see a glimmer of light on the first floor — a light that shone from behind a window with a drawn blind. For an instant the moving shadow of a heavily built man was visible.

'I think that is Burgin's shadow,' said Quest softly. 'I wonder what's going on in there.'

He left his partner standing by the wall. He himself wanted to have a look round the grounds before attempting to break into the house. He was gone for some time, and Lester began to get anxious.

'I have been all over the garden,' he said when he eventually returned,' and there is no one about. I've unlocked the gate, just in case we need to get out that way in a hurry. And now I'm going to try and get in. You stay exactly where you are. Don't worry about me. I shall be all right.'

To enter that house of unknown horror, where Pierre Renault and George Dawe had so mysteriously disappeared, was a thing that called for extreme courage.

Quest fully realised the terrible risk he was taking, but he did not shrink from it. Risks would have to be taken if ever Dr. Burgin's crimes were to be brought to light, and that was what Philip Quest was determined to bring about.

Having glanced at the upper window and seen that the light was still burning there, he crept noiselessly to the rear of the dwelling, expecting to have some difficulty in getting in.

On trying the kitchen door, however, he found to his surprise that it was unlocked. The discovery did not cause him any apprehension. He was sure that a trap had not been set for him. Probably the door had been left unlocked by carelessness, he reflected, as he softly opened it and glided into the room.

He was thoroughly familiar with the house, as he had searched it twice. Groping in the darkness he made his way to a narrow passage, and from that to the front of the main hall, where he stopped at the foot of the staircase.

And now, as he was listening with strained ears, his heart gave a quick jump. He heard faint, rustling sounds. Somebody was coming quietly, stealthily down the stairs. Was it the doctor? Or was it Prantz, the servant? Or was it a burglar, who had managed to break into the house?

Quest was in a dilemna. What should he do. Should he beat a retreat or stand his ground. He moved aside and crouched by the wall, trusting he would not be discovered, and he had just shifted his position when he was startled by a loud thumping noise.

The descending person had slipped or stumbled, and was falling. He landed with a thud at the bottom of the stairs, and scrambled to his feet, and in doing so lurched against Quest.

The next instant the two were struggling, Immediately a door on the landing above was thrown open. By the light from within, which streamed down to the hall, Quest saw Burgin and his servant rush out. And in the light, to their mutual bewilderment, the detective and his assailant recognised each other.

'Quest!' gasped the one.

'Ferris! Thank God!' exclaimed the detective, and the relief in his voice was like a sob.

11

What Ferris Overheard

There was no time to waste in questions. As soon as they spoke a shot was fired. The bullet narrowly missed Quest and a second grazed Ferris' arm as they took to their heels. They raced to the rear of the hall, and safely reached the kitchen, Dr. Burgin and his servant tearing after them.

Robert Ferris, was in the lead. He darted out into the garden, but Quest, on an impulse, stood a little to one side of the hall doorway, and waited.

Oscar Prantz was the first to hurry into the kitchen. Quest let him go by, seeing that he was unarmed, and when he saw Dr. Burgin appear almost immediately afterwards he let fly at him with his fist, and dealt him a heavy blow on the chin that sent him crashing to the floor.

'That will settle you!' he muttered, as he rubbed his sore knuckles, for the blow had been a hard one.

The doctor was half-dazed. He made a feeble effort to rise, and sank down again. He had not seen who had struck him, for the kitchen was in darkness.

Thinking only of escape now, Quest hastened outside and found a lively fight on. Robert Ferris and Lester were struggling with Oscar Prantz. All three were on the ground. Quest flashed his torch, found Oscar Prantz, and in a second had landed on him. The fight did not last much longer. The other two scrambled to their feet, and Quest, who had the advantage of the servant, sent two smashing blows on his jaw. This, as he had intended, put the servant right out, he lay like a log.

'Come along,' called the detective. 'We've got to run for it.'

They promptly took to flight, racing round to the front of the house and out at the gate. To their relief Lime Grove was deserted, and dashing out, they turned into a side street and sped on.

Faintly they heard Dr. Burgin calling, and the sound of a policeman's whistle.

The sound was behind them, however, they had nothing to fear.

When they had put a fair distance between themselves and Lime Grove they stopped running. Fortunately, crawling along just in front of them, on the main road, was a taxi, and the man at the wheel responded to Quest's whistle. He gave the driver the address in the city.

'What a night!' said Robert Ferris, when they were seated in the taxi. 'I owe you my life, Quest. But for you I would have been caught. I couldn't possibly have got away.'

'I don't think you could,' said Quest.

'I'm certain of it! How the devil did you know I was in the house?'

'I had good reason to believe you were there, Ferris. I thought you had been murdered, though. I was amazed when the light showed me who I was struggling with.'

'No more amazed than I was. You were the last person on earth I expected to find there. So you broke in to search for my dead body.'

'I did, not that I was hopeful of finding

it. I quite thought you had vanished, like Renault and Dawe.'

Quest briefly related everything, beginning with an account of the daring abduction of David Morley from the Regal Mansions, and the happy sequel to it, and going on to speak of the telephone message he had received from the young man, of the trick that had been played at Scotland Yard, and of what he had learned from the constable in Lime Grove.

By the time he had finished the narrative the taxi was drawing up outside Quest's offices. They went through to the consulting room, and Lester poured out each a drink. Seated in comfort, and with a plentiful supply of cigarettes on the small table that stood between the detective's chair and the settee that held Ferris and Lester, the Scotland Yard man, told his story.

'My patience was at an end,' he began. 'Very little had been accomplished, in spite of your efforts and mine, and I felt that I couldn't let matters rest as they were any longer. It was with a desperate resolve in my mind, in the hope of getting some tangible evidence against Dr. Burgin that I went to St. John's Wood tonight. I had been waiting outside for a little time before the constable came along, and I had a few words with him, as you know, and soon after he left me I climbed over the wall into the grounds of Number 6.

'I got into the house by forcing a small window open, and when I had unlocked the door, to provide a quick means of escape, I made my way to the front hall, and crept up to the stairs to the side of the laboratory. A light was burning inside and the doctor and his servant were in there talking. I listened for a considerable time, until I heard the doctor say he was going to bed.

'Then I left, and as ill-luck would have it, I slipped while I was descending the stairs, and fell to the bottom. As soon as I had got to my feet I stumbled into you, and I thought I had got hold of one of Burgin's men. You don't know how near I came to shooting you, Quest. I was pulling a pistol from my pocket when the light shone on us from above.'

Robert Ferris paused for a moment.

'Though I can't be sure,' he continued, 'I'm strongly inclined to think that what I learned will prove to be well worth the risk I took. And I daresay you will agree with me.

'I was not able to hear all the conversation between Burgin and his servant, but I heard a great deal of it. Two things in particular were very interesting. It appears, for one thing, that one of the doctor's friends in London, an Austrian by the name of Lubner, has been sent to Berlin to purchase certain chemicals, which apparently can only be had in that city.'

Quest raised his eyebrows.

'To purchase chemicals?' he repeated.

'Yes, that's right.'

'When did the man leave for Berlin?'

'I don't know, Quest.'

'When do they expect him back?'

'That I don't know, either.'

'Go on, Ferris. What else did you hear?'

'Something that related to you. Dr. Burgin spoke of the night of the second search of his house, and of the ancient manuscript dealing with the Black Arts that fell out of the cabinet in the library. 'I am glad Mr. Quest did not accept my offer to let him read it,' he said to Oscar Prantz. 'Had he done so he might have been shrewd enough to grasp the significance of certain passages.' He also said to the servant that you were doubtless not aware of the fact that there was a copy of the same manuscript in the Marazine Library in Paris.'

'No, I was not,' Quest remarked. 'So there is another copy of the treatise on Black Arts in existence — eh? I must have a look at that.'

'Do you really think it will be worth a visit to Paris?' asked Robert Ferris.

'From what the doctor said I should certainly think so. What with that and the purchase of chemicals from Berlin, we may be able to clear up this mystery. This throws a light on things, and confirms my suspicions. Some days ago I worked this all out, from the body-snatching at the Samaritan Hospital, to the disappearance of Dawe, and the result was so horrible that I didn't care to dwell on it.'

'What was it?' asked Robert Ferris, and

Lester leaned forward with an eager look.

'That,' said Philip Quest, 'I am not prepared to tell you — yet. If I am wrong, then no harm has been done. And if I am right then — ' He paused for a moment. 'Well, then you'll know for yourselves.'

And that was all he would say about his theory.

'Did you hear anything else, Ferris? Did Burgin speak of Pierre Renault, or of George Dawe?'

'No, not either of them.'

'Of David Morley?'

'I believe I heard his name mentioned. I think I also heard Juan Ramenez's name.'

'Was there any mention of you?'

'Yes, there was an indirect reference to the trick that was played at Scotland Yard tonight. The doctor told Oscar Prantz that I would probably be in the Thames by tomorrow, and that his next step would be to have you disposed of. He said that we were both getting too dangerous.'

Quest smiled grimly.

'Is that so? That's a compliment to us.

The old snake is afraid that we will draw his sting, is he? We will, too, in the end.'

'I have my doubts,' Robert Ferris replied. 'We've done more harm than good, tonight. Dr. Burgin will increase his vigilance, and his efforts. If he didn't recognise you and me his servant did.'

'Don't worry. We will increase our vigilance and efforts.'

'Another thing, Quest, the doctor will take it for granted that we came together, and that we overheard his conversation with Prantz.'

Quest nodded gravely.

'Yes, that is serious,' he said. 'Burgin will see that we don't have a chance to intercept the man from Berlin with the chemicals. And he will, of course, presume that I will pay a visit to the Marazine Library. Can you imagine how he is feeling at the moment. I'll bet he's in a rage. I wonder — ' He broke off and laughed. 'The doctor would love to have us arrested for housebreaking, but that's the last thing he can do. His audacity won't carry him to that length, Ferris. We needn't be alarmed, but we'll have to be very careful — and clever.'

They talked on and on, far into the night, discussing the state of affairs, and what steps they should take next. Quest made the decision on that.

It was daylight when Robert Ferris decided to go, the excitement of the night had died, and he was feeling tired.

'Well, that's settled,' he said. 'I'll send a couple of men to watch Dr. Burgin's house, with instructions not to go too close, and to keep together as much as possible. Tomorrow night Lester goes to Cresswell Road, collects David Morley and takes him to a place of safety, and you are going to Paris. When you return you will keep an eye on Juan Ramenez. That is the programme?'

'Exactly!' said Quest. 'That is all we can do — at least for the present. If we succeed in tripping the doctor up, Ferris, as eventually we shall,' he added, 'it will not be by direct proof of murders he has committed. It will be by learning what horrible secret he possesses, and by what fiendish means he has disposed of the bodies of his victims!'

12

A Daring Abduction

Between nine and ten o'clock on the following night Richard Lester called at the residence of David Morley in Beverly Street. He came out shortly afterwards carrying a suitcase, and when he had walked for some distance, to make sure that no one was following him, he picked up a taxi and was driven to Mr. Renoff's house in Cresswell Road.

He enquired for David Morley and was shown, by a servant, into the library, where the young man was reading. He was prepared for the visit, for Quest had telephoned him that morning, telling him that his partner would call later, but not stating anything further.

'Have you been out of Town?' he asked, eyeing the suitcase.

Lester shook his head.

'No, I brought this for you,' he replied.

'You are going out of town, and I am going with you.'

Morley looked surprised, but Lester took no notice and continued.

'I've just been to your house and had the butler fill the case with what I thought you would need. Mr. Quest has gone to Paris on business, and he told me to take you down to West Wycombe. We shall stay at a comfortable inn. It's a nice old place. You'll like it.'

'I thought I could stay here,' said David Morley. 'It's quite safe. Why have I got to leave? Don't tell me I am in danger again?'

'It isn't that. Mr. Quest thinks you ought to be out of London for a time.'

'All right. I suppose he knows best.'

'You bet he does!' said Lester. 'When Philip Quest says 'do this,' we do it.'

David Morley smiled. He liked this young man, and he knew that the detective would not have sent him had he not had good reason.

'Any fresh news?' he asked. 'Has anything happened since yesterday?'

'Plenty. I'll tell you what it is on the way down. The train leaves at ten-thirty, from Marylebone. It is a quarter to, now, so we haven't much time to spare.'

'We needn't start at once, then. I must write a note for Carol and her father. They have gone to a theatre. They wanted me to go with them, but much as I would have liked to I didn't care to take the risk.'

The letter was written and put in a conspicuous place on the library table. Morley went upstairs to get his outdoor clothes, and in a quarter of an hour they were ready to leave the house. In the hall the young man stopped.

'Before we go,' he said, 'I'd like to have a few words with you. I know Mr. Quest would not send me into the country unless there was some strong reason for it. Don't try and deceive me. Tell me the truth.'

'Yes, there is a reason,' assented Lester. 'Mr. Quest is afraid you won't be safe here long, because Juan Ramenez has met Miss Renoff, and he knows she is engaged to you. Ramenez would have told Dr. Burgin, of course, and when the doctor has satisfied himself that you are not at your home or with Mr. Quest it will occur to him that you are staying with Mr. Renoff.'

'Yes, of course. I wonder I didn't think of it!' replied David Morley. 'Is anybody watching your place in the city.'

'Not as far as we know. I don't think so.'

'And for that reason Quest is afraid my enemies are watching this house, Lester?'

'He doesn't think they are as yet, but he fears they will, though.'

'Well, I'm glad Mr. Quest thought of the danger. If he hadn't I might have been kidnapped again.'

The young man was willing enough to go now. They left the house together, and after glancing furtively in all directions, turned the corner into Queen's Gate and walked towards Kensington Road, searching for a taxi.

They had gone only a short distance when a closed car, dark in colour, glided slowly by from the rear and stopped several yards in front of them. A tall, well dressed man got out, followed by a second one.

At the same moment, just as a suspicion of danger flashed to Lester's mind, he heard stealthy footsteps behind him. Before he could turn he was struck down by a blow on the head, and his senses swam at once into oblivion.

★　★　★

When Lester came back to consciousness, his head aching from the blow, he was inside of the car, with his wrists tied and a hadkerchief bound across his mouth.

There were four other persons in the car, as he could see by the dim light there was. A man sat on each side of him, and on the opposite seat, also between two men, was David Morley. He was in a limp, relaxed attitude. He appeared to be still insensible, even looked as though he had been drugged.

No sound of traffic could be heard. All was quiet, except for the throbbing noise of the car. It was clearly not running over a paved road, and Lester had no doubt that they were already some where in the country. He could not see outside, for he was sitting with his back to the chauffeur, and the blinds were drawn.

What had happened was obvious. Four of Dr. Burgin's agents had been watching the house in Cresswell Road. They had seen him leave with David Morley, and the men had shadowed them from the house to Queen's Gate, two in the car and two on foot.

Lester wondered where they were being taken. It couldn't be to the house at St. John's Wood. Dr. Burgin would never risk that. More than likely they were on the way to Doomesday House. He had promised to let his partner know as soon as they arrived at West Wycombe, and he knew that if Quest did not hear from him he would know that something had happened and start searching for them. There were only two places to search. Doomesday House and the house in Lime Grove, but, Quest had gone to Paris, and the soonest he would be back would be two to three days, and anything might happen in that time, they might even be murdered. Lester shuddered at the thought.

It was a long ride, hour after hour seemed to pass, and still the car rushed steadily on. The men did not speak to one another, nor did they speak to the two men they had kidnapped. Also David Morley remained in the same half comatose state, his chin sunk on his breast.

A pale light seemed to struggle through the blinds of the windows, and when the car eventually stopped and one of the men opened the door it was fully daylight.

Lester was thrust roughly out. Looking round quickly, he saw to his dismay, that he was not in Essex, the landscape was very different, and there was no sign of a house.

The man who had stepped from the car was a sinister looking fellow, with sandy hair and a big moustache. He untied the young man's wrists and took the handkerchief from his mouth.

'We are setting you free,' he said, with quite a foreign accent, 'to show you that we have no fear of you. It is your companion we want, not you. In a quarter of an hour from now David Morley will be on a private yacht which is lying yonder at the coast. Before the day is over he will be in France, and it will be useless to search for him. Go back to London and tell what I have told you to that foolish detective who has meddled in affairs that do not concern him, and be thankful that your life has been spared.'

The man got into the car, and it glided rapidly away, carrying David Morley to an unknown fate, and disappeared over a crest of high ground.

'Poor fellow,' said Lester to himself. 'I'm afraid that's the last we shall see of him.'

He had not the least idea where he was. He was on a lonely deserted road, and in an unfamiliar part of the country. On all sides of him, as far as the eye could reach, were rolling wooded hills, and meadows in which sheep were grazing. There was no human being, no habitation, anywhere in sight.

The breeze that was blowing had a salty tang to it. He knew the coast must be somewhere near. The car had gone that way, but it was useless to attempt to trace it.

Choosing what he judged would be the best course to take, he set off in the opposite direction, towards the glow of the rising sun. Hungry and thirsty, sick at heart, depressed by the thought of what would happen to Morley, he trudged for a couple of miles along the lonely road, meeting nobody.

Presently he heard the sound of a train in the distance, and shortly afterwards, coming to the top of a hill, he saw directly below him a small village and a railway station.

He had not been robbed by his captors. He had money in his pocket. He tramped down the hill and stopped at the village inn, where they told him he was about ten miles from Bridport, in Dorset. He enquired about the train service, and was informed that there was a local train leaving in an hour that would take him to Dorchester, from which station he could get an express to Paddington. The landlady looked at him suspiciously. Strangers were rare in this quiet little place. And certainly Lester did invite comment. He was tired, and his neat suit was badly creased, from the cramped journey in the car.

He had a wash and a good breakfast, and then set off for the station. The local train was slow, but eventually it reached Dorchester. Once in the express Lester slept, and only wakened as the train was pulling into the platform in London.

It was late afternoon when he reached home, but Philip Quest had not yet returned from his Paris trip.

13

The Parcel

It is possible that, had not Philip Quest been compelled to alter his plans, his visit to Paris would have been uneventful. He had intended to make the journey by aeroplane, but as he was rather late in starting from the city, and as the taxi was held up twice in traffic blocks, he got to Croydon just five minutes too late.

He did not feel inclined to charter a special machine, so he drove back to Victoria and caught the afternoon boat-train, travelled by Dover and Boulogne, and arrived in Paris that night at about the time when Richard Lester was leaving David Morley's residence in Beverly Street with the suitcase.

He went to a quiet hotel, and the next morning, after breakfast, he took a taxi to the Marazine Library.

The library, with its half a million

volumes and many thousands of manuscripts was housed in the Institut de France, and was originally founded by Cardinal Marazine in the sixteenth century.

Dr. Burgin had not been mistaken. The ancient manuscript treating of the Black Arts was here, and the librarian found it with little difficulty. Quest saw at a glance that it was a copy precisely similar to the one he had seen in the doctor's library.

He carried it to a table, and read it from beginning to end, the while he made occasional notes. The old Italian script was not very legible, and his task occupied him for more than an hour.

He left the Institute feeling that he had been well rewarded for his trouble, and was walking along the Quai Malaquais, absorbed in thought, and with rather a startled look in his eyes, when, an open cab approached rapidly from behind him. He did not notice it, but as it was gliding by he heard a muffled report, and a bullet whistled close to his ear.

The shot had come from the cab, in which was seated a man whose features were not visible to the detective. He fired a second shot, and again in his haste he missed. The cab dashed on, swerving to the right, and Quest lost sight of it.

That it had been a deliberate attempt of murder there was no doubt. Even here, it seemed, Dr. Burgin had his spies. Quest knew that he would have to be very careful if he was to get out of France alive.

Apparently no one had observed the incident. The noise of the traffic had prevented the two shots being heard. Though the cab was probably on the other side of the Seine, by now, the detective prudently turned in the opposite direction. He picked up a taxi and instructed the driver to take him to his hotel, but by a circuitous route.

He had been very near to death but his nerves were not shaken. He was savagely indignant, in a towering rage, and it would have gone hard with the would-be assassin had he been able to get his hands on him.

He was at no loss to account for what had occurred. It was capable of only one explanation, as he had no enemies in the French capital, in fact it is doubtful if anybody, other than his partner and Ferris, knew that he had made this journey. He must have been shadowed from the city to Croydon, and from Croydon to Victoria; followed to Paris, and subsequently been kept under surveillance.

'They must have seen me go into the Institut,' he reflected, 'and waited for me to come out.'

Philip Quest's conjectures were right. Dr. Francis Burgin had wasted no time in having the detective watched. Ever since the disappearance of George Dawe his movements had been followed with great care, and since the night he and Ferris had been discovered in his house at Lime Grove the doctor had determined to get rid of them. That Quest would go to Paris to have a look at the treatise on the Black Arts he had no doubt, and the man detailed to keep him in sight had been instructed to follow him wherever he should go, and should he visit the Institut to make sure that he would not come back to London with whatever knowledge he had gained there. In one paragraph of the treatise was a clue, so cunningly worded, so deftly phrased, that the veiled and subtle meaning might be easily misconstrued, but Burgin knew that the detective was a shrewd and clever man, and would find in that folio the secret of the happenings in London. Therefore it was imperative that Quest should not return to make that knowledge public.

On arriving at his hotel Philip Quest saw at once that something was amiss.

Groups of people were talking in the lounge and he caught a word or two about an attempt on somebody's life. As he entered the bureau the manager hastened towards him.

'It was most fortunate that you were absent, monsieur!' he exclaimed. 'You have had a narrow escape from death!'

'A narrow escape?' repeated Quest. 'What on earth do you mean?'

'It is terrible!' said the excited manager. 'Had you been here you would probably have been killed.'

'Calm yourself,' said the detective. 'I

don't know what you are talking about. Would you mind explaining?'

The manager eagerly began the story.

'A parcel came for you, monsieur,' he said. 'It was apparently a cardboard-box, seven or eight inches in length, wrapped in paper and sealed with wax. It was handed to me at the desk. I sent the hall porter with it to your room. He was in a hurry, and entering your room tripped over a rug. He dropped the parcel, and at once there was an explosion, and a burst of flame which gave out suffocating fumes. Happily the door and windows were open and the draught blew the fumes out into the air. But the porter inhaled enough of them to make him unconscious, however, and it was some minutes before he recovered.'

'Was he badly hurt?' asked Quest.

'No,' replied the manager. 'He has a bad head, that is all.'

'Is anything left of the parcel?'

'No, it was destroyed. There are only some fragments of blackened glass, and a charred cork.'

'Who brought it here?'

'A boy who was a stranger to me, monsieur.'

'How long ago?'

'Less than half an hour. I have not yet informed the police. I will do so now. They will discover — '

'No, no,' said Quest hastily. 'Don't report the matter. No serious harm has been done, and I don't want to be detained here. I must return to London today.'

The manager reluctantly consented, and Quest went upstairs to his room, where he saw a burnt spot on the carpet.

'A stupid trick,' he murmured. 'I certainly should not have been so foolish as to open the parcel.'

He surmised that the man who had fired the two shots at him in the street was responsible for this second attempt on his life. Apparently he had had two strings to his bow, and when he found that his first attempt had failed had immediately gone to the hotel and sent in the parcel.

Now that he had been to the Marazine Library there was nothing else to keep him in Paris. He went downstairs with his bag, paid his bill and departed. He drove to Le Bourget in a taxi, and he was satisfied, when he arrived there, that he had not been followed.

Quest was fortunate in getting a seat in an air liner that was soon to leave, and when he got home, towards the evening, he found Lester waiting for him.

The young man told his story, and Quest was greatly upset by the disastrous news. It was the hardest kind of blow to him. He felt that the ground had been cut from beneath his feet.

For some minutes he did not speak, but paced the floor like a caged lion, his face a mixture of fury and distress.

'So Dr. Burgin has scored again, eh?' he said bitterly. 'This is most discouraging.'

'I feel as badly about it as you do,' said Lester. 'Poor Morley! What chance have we of finding him on the Continent!'

Suddenly the detective stopped his pacing of the room and turned to his young partner.

'I don't think Morley is on the

Continent,' he said. 'I don't believe that story of the yacht. That drive to Dorset was a blind, to throw us off the scent. Had the sea been their real destination they would not have told you. They set you free for the same reason, thinking I would credit what you were told to tell me.'

'Perhaps that was the reason,' said Lester. 'It didn't occur to me before. Do you think they drove back to town with Morley? Where can he be? I don't think they would have taken him to St. John's Wood. And it's not likely that he is at Doomesday House.'

'No, I don't suppose he is at either place. He can't have been taken to Lime Grove, for the house is being watched day and night, and you would have had a message had anything suspicious happened there.'

'What will they do with him? Do you think his life is in danger?'

'I don't know. I am as much in the dark as you. To be perfectly candid, Lester, I don't think we shall ever see him again. I could tell you more if I knew what Dr.

Burgin and Juan Ramenez have to gain by getting the young man in their power. Possibly it will be to their interest to keep him alive, though I should hardly think so.'

Quest dropped the subject and briefly told his partner of the two attempts to murder him that had been made in Paris.

'The doctor had very good reasons to try to prevent me from seeing the manuscript in the Marazine Library,' he said.

'You haven't told me anything about that yet,' said Lester. 'Was it in the library?'

'Yes, it was there. And I read it from beginning to end.'

'Was it worth reading,' asked Lester eagerly.

'Well worth it,' replied Quest. 'I got information of great value relating to the Black Arts, and a clue to the mystery — to Dr. Burgin's ghastly secret. It supports what I vaguely suspected. But it is so dreadful that I would rather not speak of it now.' I shudder at the thought of it.'

'Tell me what it is?' begged Lester. 'I am curious.'

Quest shook his head. He did not want to discuss this horrible thing with Lester. As yet he had no actual proof that he could put before a jury, and until he had it was better that he alone should know the secret of Lime Grove and the disappearance of the two men.

'I am losing patience,' he said. 'Something must be done. I told you the other night, if Doctor Burgin is to be laid by the heels it must be by knowing how he contrived to dispose of the bodies of his victims. I shall consult Sir John Carfax, the Chief Commissioner of Police. I will put all the facts in my possession before him, and tell him of my theories and suspicions, and ask him to grant a warrant for the arrest of the doctor. If he consents I will be able to find out just what chemicals and appliances are in the laboratory of Number 6, Lime Grove. That will help me a lot.'

Philip Quest rose.

'I am going to Scotland Yard now,' he said. 'I want a few minutes talk with

Robert Ferris. And by the way, Lester, I don't think we'll tell the Renoffs of the abduction of David Morley. Let them think, for the present, that he is safe at West Wycombe.'

14

Dr. Burgin Disappears

Philip Quest had a restless night. Anxiety for David Morley preyed on his mind, and apart from that, although he was not discouraged, he was beginning to fear that the wily doctor might win through in the end.

'I shall go to see the Chief Commissioner today,' he said to Lester at breakfast the next morning. 'And I shall want you to keep an eye on Juan Ramenez. He has been neglected too long. It is possible that — '

There was a rap at the door and Robert Ferris came into the room. There was a troubled look on his face.

'Sorry to disturb you so early, Quest,' he said.

'You have some news for me?' enquired the detective.

'Yes, and it's not very good.'

'What is it? Please don't tell me that another of your men have fallen into the clutches of — '

'No. Dr. Burgin has disappeared.'

'Disappeared?' echoed Quest. 'How?'

'By a very simple manœuvre,' said Robert Ferris. 'It was the last thing I anticipated, and I was not prepared for it. After you had left the Yard last night I went to St. John's Wood and relieved one of the two men who were on duty. About nine o'clock an empty taxi stopped in front of Number 6. It must have been ordered by telephone, for presently Dr. Burgin and his servant came out of the house, got into the cab, and drove away. I followed them in another cab, which I had waiting round the corner. Both left the taxi at Piccadilly Circus and separated. Oscar Prantz walked towards Leicester Square and the doctor went into the Café Royal. I went in also, and kept a discreet eye on him. He sat there for half an hour, sipping a whisky and soda, and reading a newspaper. When he left he strolled over to Swan & Edgar's corner, across Piccadilly turned down Lower

Regent Street and paused a little beyond Jermyn Street, close to a car that was standing at the edge of the pavement. He lit a cigar, and then, at a moment when the roadway was clear of traffic, he suddenly whipped into the car. It glided off at once in the direction of Waterloo Place, and as the man who was driving turned his head to look behind him, I recognised Oscar Prantz.

'I knew it would be too late to give chase to them by the time I had found a taxi, so I drove to Lime Grove, thinking they may have returned there. They had not. I instructed the man on duty to stay there all night, and an hour ago, after he had been relieved by another man, he got through to me on the telephone and reported that Dr. Burgin and his servant were still absent.'

He paused and looked at Quest.

'What do you make of it? A slap in the face for us, eh?'

Quest nodded gravely.

'Yes, it leaves us at a loose end,' he said. 'For some reason — it can hardly be that he is alarmed — the doctor has judged it advisable to disappear for a while. He had his plans cut and dried last night when he set off with his servant. He took it for granted that he would be under observation, of course. That is why he left the servant and went into the Café Royal. In the meanwhile Oscar Prantz got a car from somewhere, probably also ordered by phone, drove to Lower Regent Street and waited there for the doctor. I'd give anything to know where they have gone.'

'If you ask me,' said Robert Ferris, 'I should say they had a yacht somewhere on the coast in readiness and have gone over to the Continent to join the men who abducted young Morley.'

'Somehow I don't think so,' said Quest. 'I told you yesterday that I haven't any faith in the tale that was poured into Lester's ears. It was meant to put me on a false scent. If they said they were going on the Continent it's ten to one they are still in England. And if David Morley is still alive Burgin is with him.'

'Perhaps they are at that house in Essex, Quest?'

'I strongly doubt it. Dr. Burgin is aware

that I know about the house in Essex, and so that would be the last place he would take him to.'

'We have little chance then of finding the poor fellow,' said Ferris.

'Hardly any,' said the detective. 'We are at a complete deadlock. As matters are we can only wait in the hope of finding some clue.'

Quest paused for a moment.

'I thought of going down to the Yard to see Carfax today, Ferris,' he continued. 'I'll put the whole thing to him. The only hope for us is to get a warrant for the arrest of Dr. Burgin. Get him out of the house, and give us the run of it and then we might be able to clear up this mystery.'

'But how on earth do you expect to get a warrant to arrest a man when you only have suspicions? You know Carfax won't do a thing like that. I see your point of view, Quest, and I know that the only way to get any concrete evidence is to get into the house, but you haven't enough proof to justify the arrest of Burgin.'

'If we have to wait for absolute proof we shall wait for ever!' said Quest with some heat. 'Haven't I tried for weeks to get proof? Don't you want to know what happened to your friend. Is the fact that he has disappeared sufficient reason to let the case drop? You asked me to look into the affair, and I'm not going to give up while there's the slightest chance of getting to the bottom of the mysteries.'

Quest was annoyed. It seemed that Ferris was content to wait, and the detective knew that the longer they waited the less chance they stood of putting a rope round the neck of Dr. Burgin.

'Well,' he continued, 'I'm going along to see Carfax. Are you coming with me?'

'Certainly,' replied Ferris. 'I was only trying to explain that you'd have a hard job to get the Commissioner to give you the warrant.'

'I'll chance it!' said Quest, and a few minutes later they left the offices.

Sir John Carfax, who was already acquainted with most of the circumstances, had a long talk with Quest and Robert Ferris that morning, and expressed the opinion that it would not be advisable to issue a warrant until stronger evidence against the doctor had been obtained. And as for the police, meanwhile, making a forced entry into the house at St. John's Wood, he simply would not hear of it.

'I won't give my consent,' he said. 'It would be a high-handed proceeding, and might be the subject of another complaint in Parliament about the liberties of the citizen.'

For over an hour they talked, but the Commissioner was adamant.

'Frankly,' he said to Quest, 'I think you have run away with yourself. Your suspicions and theories are impossible. Fantastic! No, Quest, you had better start at the beginning and go over the whole affair again. I think there is another explanation of the disappearances.'

'Well, what?' asked the detective.

'I don't know,' answered the Chief Commissioner. 'I'm not on the case. But never-the-less, you'll have to bring me something more solid than suspicions before I can grant you the warrant.'

So Philip Quest was not to have a chance of verifying his suspicions which the treatise on the Black Arts planted in his mind. He left Scotland Yard much disappointed and not a little angry.

He returned to the City for lunch and told Lester of the interview.

'We will just have to go ahead on our own,' he said. 'I think, Lester, that you had better go down to Essex again, and for goodness sake be careful.'

As before Richard Lester travelled by rail and took his bicycle with him, and when he got back that night he brought information with him that was discouraging to the detective.

By enquiries at Durling Wood he had learned that Dr. Burgin's servant, the man Hodge, was for the present staying with a married sister in the neighbourhood, and that he had stated that the doctor had gone abroad, and was not likely to return to England for some time.

Lester had subsequently cycled over to Doomesday House and prowled about the house for several hours, and he was positive, he declared, that no one was living there.

During the next two days the situation remained exactly the same, and Quest was like a bear with a sore head. Lester secretly sympathised with him, for he knew how helpless the detective felt. They knew nothing, and there was not a clue to the whereabouts of the doctor. Two men from the Yard were still keeping a watch on the house in St. John's Wood, but neither the doctor or his servant had returned.

The watch on Juan Ramenez's movements were barren of result. The Spanish gentleman kept no rendezvous with any suspicious character.

Dover, Folkestone, and Harwich were advised to watch for the man Lubner, as were the airports at Croydon and Heston, but he did not arrive. And nothing was heard of David Morley.

On the morning of the third day a letter was delivered to Quest. It had been posted at St. Malo, on the coast of Brittany, and it ran as follows:

'I trust, My dear Mr. Quest, that you are not taking my absence too much to heart. You are engaged on other professional pursuits, perhaps, which will do more credit to your skill than your futile attempts to prove that I am a monster of iniquity. I regret that private business compelled me to go abroad and leave you at a loose end. I am shortly returning to London, however, and should you be disposed to renew your efforts, you will find me domiciled in Lime Grove again. But believe me you will be well advised if you cease to interest yourself in my affairs in future.'

It bore no signature.

Quest had read the letter aloud.

'It's from Burgin, of course,' he remarked to Lester, a note of anger in his voice. 'The insolent scoundrel! He'll sing a different tune before I have finished with him!'

★ ★ ★

Philip Quest shut himself up in the consulting room for the rest of the morning, trying to think out exactly where Dr. Burgin could be. His intuition told him that Burgin was not out of the country. That story of the yacht he had never believed, and now this letter from Brittany could not convince him. In trying to assure Quest that he was abroad the doctor had made a false move. He had only succeeded in making the detective more certain than ever that he was not far away. The clever doctor had been a little too clever. Quest was certain now that Dr. Burgin was only playing for time; that David Morley was alive, and that the doctor had spared his life because he was waiting for something — probably the man from Berlin. Had the doctor been abroad he would have had no reason to write to Quest or attempt to deceive him, for he would know that he could not be found.

Then where could he be? There was only one place, and that was at Doomesday House. Quest was beginning to feel more hopeful by the time luncheon was announced. He told Lester of his theories concerning the whereabouts of the Doctor and informed him that they were going to Essex that day.

'But there is nobody there,' said the young man. 'I went right round the place and there wasn't a sign of anybody.'

'All the same, to Doomesday House we're going!'

15

The Man From Berlin

Though his belief was based on nothing more substantial than deductions, Quest was confident that the end of the sensational case was at last in sight.

He went straight to Scotland Yard, saw Robert Ferris, and arranged with him to be ready to act on receipt of a message. Late in the afternoon he and Lester set off for Essex in the car.

Giving the village of Durling Wood a wide berth they drove by a circuitous route almost as far as the sea, and doubling back they held to a lonely road that crossed the flat, green marshes, and brought them to a plantation that was within half a mile of Dr. Burgin's country house.

They had glimpsed the roof of it as they approached, but they could not see it now, for the sun was below the horizon, and it was growing dark.

They ran the car in amongst the trees and Quest got out. He had a loaded automatic in his pocket, and also a pair of wire cutters, which he judged he would need.

'You have your instructions, Lester,' he said, 'and I will depend on you not to disregard them. It is just seven o'clock. If I don't return in two hours you will know I have been caught, and without delay drive up to town, report to Robert Ferris, and tell him to make haste.'

'And what do I do should I hear pistol shots while I am waiting?' asked Lester.

'In that event give me half an hour,' replied Quest, 'and if I am not back by then you will dash off to Scotland Yard. If I do get into trouble you will not be able to help me, and I don't want you to try.'

'I am afraid you will get into trouble,' replied the young man. 'I do wish you'd let me come with you.'

'No, you've got to stay here. If we were both to be caught there would be no hope of rescue — or very little. Robert Ferris would wait until tomorrow morning before he would take any steps.'

Lester remained in the car, and Quest departed on his adventure. He was taking his life in his hands, he knew, but without that risk nothing would be accomplished. He knew what precautions he meant to observe, and he trusted that they would protect him from pitfalls.

Keeping his bearings as best he could he worked round in a detour, sheltered by woods all the way; and in a quarter of an hour he stumbled on a footpath that led him to the rear of Doomesday House, where there was a small gate.

Finding it to be locked, as he had expected, he used his wire cutters to clip a quantity of prickly foliage from the bottom of the hedge in which the gate was set, and in this way made a narrow gap. With some little trouble he managed to squeeze his body through and at last found himself in the garden.

All was quiet. Not a sound reached his ears, and he could not detect the faintest glimmer of light anywhere. He was not discouraged, however, he knew that the doctor was too clever to give any hint of his presence once he had stated that he was not in residence.

Dropping on his hands and knees, he stole forward amongst the trees and shrubbery, moving very slowly and very stealthily, peering into the gloom beyond him, and feeling in the grass for concealed wires.

In the course of twenty minutes he had gone entirely round the house, and was back at the rear of it again. The place was absolutely in darkness, not a light from top to bottom, and he had not heard even the murmur of a voice.

Surely, he thought, if Dr. Burgin was here, a light would show somewhere at this hour of the evening. But knowing the cunning of the man Quest was not satisfied yet.

Once more he crawled to the front of the house, and crouched by a clump of bushes at the edge of the lawn. For nearly half an hour he waited there, amidst unbroken silence, and finally he was forced to the conclusion that he was wrong. There was nobody at Doomesday House. The place was deserted. He would go back to the car and return to town.

He did not want to go back and confess his mistake. Another fifteen minutes wouldn't hurt. He would stay — just in case.

Five minutes; ten minutes; And then his sharp ears caught something, a muffled cough!

With every nerve alert Quest waited, but nothing more could he hear. But he knew he had not been wrong. There was somebody in that house.

Suddenly, as he was gazing above him, something that glowed like coal fire dropped on to the lawn, close where he was hiding. It was the burning end of a cigar, and it had been thrown from an upper window.

The detective's heart gave a quick throb. He was right. Dr. Burgin was there and his servant. Probably David Morley was with them, perhaps and also the men who had been helping the doctor in his attempts to get Morley. They were there in the dark waiting — waiting — for what?

Philip Quest crept away, still on his hands and knees. At length he rose to his feet and he was gliding along one side of the house when he was startled by a lusty shout. Keen eyes had observed him from a window.

He took to his heels and was dashing towards the rear of the garden when a taut wire tripped and threw him, and a gun to which the wire was attached roared in his ears.

He was not hit. The charge had narrowly missed him. He jumped up and ran on, and he had got nearly to the gap in the hedge when he stepped on to a steel trap that was hidden in the grass and the jaws of it clutched his ankle in a grip like a vice.

He was a helpless prisoner, for the trap was chained to a stake in the ground. He could not tear the chain from it, nor could he get his ankle free, hard though he tried.

A shrill clamour was ringing now. Doors were flung open and rapid footsteps were heard. Quest floundered to and fro, making rapid efforts to escape, until his foot caught on the stake and he fell heavily.

There was only one thing for him to do, and that was fight. Shadowy forms, half a dozen in number, were hastening towards him. Lying flat on the grass, he whipped his automatic from his pocket and fired.

There was a cry of agony and the noise of a fall. He fired two more shots, aiming blindly. Both missed, for the men had taken to cover now.

'Close in on him!' shouted the voice of Dr. Burgin. 'He's in the trap! I think it's Philip Quest, or that damn partner of his!'

'Be careful, Doctor,' shouted somebody else. 'Don't show yourselves. He's killed Lowther!'

The men were still approaching, stealing from tree to tree, from bush to bush, and as they came they fired a spluttering volley of pistol shots. The bullets whistled over Quest's head, barely missing him. He discharged his automatic again, resolved to fight until the very end.

Soon the firing ceased, and there was hushed silence. Nothing could be seen moving. Nothing was heard.

The ominous silence lasted for several minutes, and then, as the detective was about to shift his position, he was suddenly pounced on by two men who had crept up behind him, and his pistol was wrenched from his hand.

For a few seconds he struggled desperately with his assailants, while blows were reigned upon him, and he was still fighting, with the men on top of him, when his senses swam into darkness. His last memory was of Dr. Burgin's face, visible in the light of a lantern.

*   *   *

It was a disheartening blow to Lester when he faintly heard the pistol shots as he was sitting in the car. He knew by that that Quest had been found and was in danger, yet he dared not go to his assistance. He had his orders and he knew that he must obey them.

After the firing had ceased he clung to a ray of hope, while he waited for half an hour, as he had been told to do; and then Quest not having returned, he decided not to wait any longer.

It was obvious that he had been caught there could be no doubt about it. Dr Burgin had got him, dead or alive. He would go to London immediately and get to Robert Ferris; perhaps, if he was not dead they might be able to rescue him in the morning.

A faint noise floated to his ears from the distance, and he recognised it as the throbbing of an aeroplane. He paid no attention to it at first, but when he heard rapid footsteps as he was preparing to start, a shrewd suspicion gripped him.

He slipped from the car, and gliding warily to the edge of the plantation, he stood in the shelter of a tree and looked beyond him. The vague figure of a man was visible, hurrying out on the open marches in the direction of the sea.

When he had gone for thirty or forty yards he stopped, lighted a lantern, and waved it two or three times.

Now the truth flashed to Lester's mind. This must mean the arrival of Lubner with the chemicals from Berlin. That Dr. Burgin had expected him tonight was apparent from the presence of the man with the lantern, who was out there flashing the light to guide the pilot.

The man with the lantern continued to wave it, while the aeroplane approached swiftly, sinking lower and lower. Twice it circled the house before it eventually came to rest, making a safe and easy landing on the grassy surface of the marsh. A man climbed down from it, carrying a large box, and greeted the man with the light.

The pilot did not get out. With the assistance of the two men he ascended again, and when they had watched the machine rise and wheel to the eastward, they came towards Lester, and passed by within a short distance of him, going in the direction of Dr. Burgin's house.

'There was a bit of a scrap about half an hour ago,' said the man with the lantern, in a voice that was quite audible to the man in the grass. 'But there is no reason to be alarmed, Lubner. It was only that cursed detective, Quest, and they caught him. It was his own fault for snooping around. I expect he's been done in by now. I hope so.'

Precious as time was Lester dared not start yet. He must be sure that the men would not hear him depart. He waited for at least twenty minutes, in a state of keen suspense, and then as quietly as possible he ran the car out of the plantation and drove as fast as he could along the road that crossed the lonely marshes.

He was greatly worried, and he would have been more worried and horrified if he had known what was taking place at Doomesday House.

16

The Horror at Doomesday House

Only for a brief period was Quest unconscious. He soon recovered, and found that he had been taken to a small bedroom. His wrists were securely bound.

His head ached abominably, due, he supposed, to the blows which the doctor's 'friends' had rained on him before he was taken prisoner.

He had no doubt as to his fate, and the thought made him feel sick. He would rather have been killed out there in the darkness than die as he knew he would. Richard Lester, he concluded, would have heard the shots and was by now hurrying to Scotland Yard to get help from Robert Ferris. But before they could possibly arrive Dr. Burgin would see that the detective had disappeared like Renault and the man Dawe.

It was his own fault for being so daring,

reflected Quest. Anyway, whatever happened, he would not give way before Burgin.

He got up and stretched himself. His head was gradually ceasing to thump and the pain across his eyes was not so bad. Perhaps, he thought, he could find a way out of this place. But a glance from the window revealed the fact that he was apparently at the top of the building, for there was a long drop to what looked like the lawn. The window also was fastened, a screw having been driven into the sash, and to attempt to break the window and jump out he knew would be madness.

His watch told him that it was nearly ten. If Lester had obeyed him he should be in town in a very short time. But what if he had not. Supposing the young man, on hearing the shots, had forgotten his instructions and rushed to help him?

The thought nearly brought him to panic. It was the kind of thing he would do, for the detective was aware that the younger man would do anything he could to help him.

The perspiration broke out on his

forehead. If that was so, then they would both die. Robert Ferris would not know until some days later, until perhaps, not having heard from them it would occur to him to telephone the offices and find out if they were there. By that time all trace of them would be gone, and even if a search warrant was granted there would be nothing in Doomesday House to show that the detective and his partner had been there.

He hoped that Lester had gone for help, not for his own sake, for once in the clutches of Dr. Burgin he well knew that he could never get out, but it would be too terrible if the young man should lose his life in trying to save his friend.

Time passed and nobody came near him. He could not hear voices or any noise that would tell him that he was not alone in that house of doom.

Quest wondered if David Morley was there, too. That he was not dead he was sure.

And then his thoughts turned again to the reason why Dr. Burgin had particularly hunted the rich young man. How could he benefit by his death? If his conjectures were right then any body, as long as it was a body, would suit the designs of the doctor, so why Morley?

The more he thought of it the more puzzled he became. He had tried, during those weeks that had elapsed since he first was interested in the affairs of David Morley, to try and find the solution, but he had failed. That there was a reason was obvious.

Well, it was no use thinking about it now. He had failed to put the rope round the neck of the doctor, and by this time, or very soon now, David Morley would be just one more man to put on the list of 'missing men'.

If only Carfax had given him that warrant, how much he could have done. By now the doctor would have been arrested, and as the man from Berlin had not arrived, they might have been able to prevent the death of Morley. The Commissioner was a very capable man in his way, but he could not, or would not, see anything that was not put under his nose. He must have proof. Proof, when only by getting into the house could they get this proof. The Commissioner thought his theories were frantic. When he, Quest, had gone the way of the others perhaps he would wake up.

He began to pace the room. This waiting was trying to his nerves. If only Burgin would come and get it over with. Probably the doctor was trying a little mental torture. Quest imagined him sitting in a comfortable room somewhere in the house gloating over the end of the man who had so nearly tripped him up. And he had nearly done so. He had found in Paris the contents of the folio in the cabinet in the library of Number 6 Lime Grove.

Again he swore at the pig-headedness of the Commissioner, who refused to arrest a man who was worse than a murderer, just because his crimes were secret.

★ ★ ★

In a room in the floor below that where Quest had been taken, Dr. Burgin sat waiting the return of his servant, Oscar Prantz. The smile on his face was not pleasant. He looked more like a maniac than a sane man.

Presently Prantz came in.

'Have you carried out my instructions, Prantz?' enquired the doctor.

'Yes, sir,' was the answer.

'And did everything go smoothly?'

'As on the former occasions, sir. It was swift and perfect work.'

'Is the other body in readiness?'

'Yes, I have seen to that.'

'Where are Lubner and Crawley?' the doctor continued.

'They are busy in the laboratory, sir,' Oscar Prantz replied.

'And the others? They are gone?'

'A quarter of an hour ago, sir. I think they were glad to get away. They haven't got your nerve.'

The doctor smiled.

'That is all for the present,' he said. 'You will help me with the next experiment, Prantz. In about half an hour come into Mr. Quest's room. I shall be there.'

Oscar Prantz departed, and immediately afterwards the doctor left his study, crossed a passage, ascended the stairs to the next landing, and entered the room where the detective was a prisoner.

Quest was expecting the visit, and had determined to appear calm whatever he may be feeling. Not doubting that his fate was sealed — he was certain that he would be dead and gone before the police could possibly arrive from Scotland Yard — he meant to maintain an interested attitude during this interview and say as little as possible.

Dr. Burgin switched on the light, seated himself in an armchair opposite the detective and put a match to a cigar.

'So you have come to this, Mr. Quest,' he remarked with a sigh, shaking his head sadly. 'You have only yourself to blame. You would not take my advice. You disregarded my friendly warning. It is a pity. A great pity, for you are a man with some admirable qualities. I am really averse to putting you out of existence. Unfortunately, however, I am compelled to do so. It is a matter of necessity. You have only a short time to live. An hour or so at the most.'

'I am quite prepared,' said Quest coolly. I understand that you must kill me because you are frightened of me. I know your secret.'

Dr. Burgin laughed softly.

'I am frightened of you?' he echoed. 'No, Mr. Quest, there you have made a mistake. I am not frightened of you. But my secret is my own. For years I have devoted my time to this work, and you are not going to cheat me out of the reward. No, I am not frightened of you.'

He leaned back and puffed for a few seconds at his cigar.

'Mr. Quest,' he continued. 'You are a brave man. You know my secret, and you are not afraid.'

'Certainly not,' declared Quest, but inwardly he shuddered.

'Excellent,' murmured the doctor. 'I hate cowards. Did you come alone to Doomesday House this evening?'

Quest did not answer, but his heart jumped. So Lester was safe. Thank goodness! As the doctor was not aware that they had come together then the young man must have followed his instructions. He would be too late to help him, but it was a great relief to know that his partner had escaped the clutches of this fiend.

Dr. Burgin had been watching him closely, and he frowned slightly.

'I may be wrong about that,' he said. 'But in any event, if you were accompanied by your partner, Richard Lester, any attempt he may make to have you rescued will be too late to succeed. You will have disappeared, and the police will find nothing here to incriminate me. Absolutely nothing.'

'It's a long lane that has no turning, doctor,' said the detective with an assumption of bravado. 'If I don't send you to the gallows somebody else will.'

'You speak of what is impossible, Mr. Quest. I shall never fall into the hands of the law, be assured. You have done your best, but you have failed. I do not fear the police. It was uncommonly clever of you, I must admit, to presume from the tale your partner was told, and from the letter

I wrote to you, that I was at my country house, and was trying to throw you on a false scent.

'By the way, I should like to know if the old manuscript you read in the Marazine Library in Paris, a copy identical with the one in my possession, gave you any clue to the means by which I contrived to deceive you on the two occasions when you searched my house in St. John's Wood?'

'Yes, it gave me a very strong clue.'

'So I supposed. And it was a natural conclusion on my part.'

Dr. Francis Burgin paused for a moment.

'You will shortly be enlightened in regard to my methods,' he resumed, 'but I will talk to you first of other matters. You tried very hard to find out about me, didn't you, Mr. Quest, but you only knew that I was Dr. Burgin, of St. John's Wood; that I spoke many languages, and that I had lived abroad most of my life. I think you will be interested to know all about me, eh? Well, I have borne many names, and not one of them was my real name. My father was a learned man, a Russian professor, and I inherited his talents. From a child I have always been interested in chemical analysis, and for science of all kinds, and it proved lucrative to me. I did not dabble in sordid crime.

'I have never been a criminal in the ordinary sense of the word. But for a number of years, while I lived on the Continent, I was consulted by international crooks, who operated on a large scale and paid me big fees. I gave them expert advice and assisted them with chemical inventions of my own and showed them how to cover up their crimes.

'So much for that. I come now to the part of my narrative which I should not dream of disclosing to you were I not certain that you will carry the secret to the grave with you, that you will have no opportunity of — '

The doctor broke off.

'No, not to your grave,' he said with an odd smile. 'There will be no last resting place for you, Mr. Quest. But to continue.

You will remember what I told you before — that several years ago, when I was searching amongst the literary treasures of an old monastery near the Italian town of Sienna, I found and purchased an ancient manuscript dealing with the Black Arts.

'At the time I had been living in St. John's Wood for about two years. When I got back to England I read the manuscript carefully and took a keen interest in the formula for manufacturing a corrosive fluid, which, the old writer stated, could be made in bulk cheaply, and would, in a very brief interval, entirely eat away a human body. I saw what boundless opportunities this offered, especially to a man of my calling. Here was a means of making murder perfectly safe, and I determined to take advantage of it if I could possibly do so.'

Dr. Burgin paused again to note the effect of his words. Though it was much what Quest had been prepared to hear, a chill of horror ran through him, and for an instant his stout courage was shaken. It would not have been necessary to tell him any more. He knew the ghastly truth now.

'But there was a difficulty in the way,' the doctor continued. 'Two of the ingredients mentioned in the formula were chemicals of which I had not the slightest knowledge. I could guess at the nature of them, however, and I was not discouraged. For many months, with dogged patience and perseverance, I worked in my laboratory. For a time it seemed as though I should never be able to succeed, but finally, no great while ago I discovered — or believed had discovered — all the chemicals of which the formula was composed. I experimented with it on a small scale, and was convinced that I had found the secret.

'The next thing was to test it on a human body. Where was I to get one? There was only one safe way. Assisted by a crook of the name of Larry Smith I broke into the mortuary of the Samaritan Hospital at White-chapel. We carried off the body of a woman. The appearance of a constable compelled us to drop it.

'Ten days later I read in a paper that

the body of an unknown man had been taken from the river, and was lying at the Rising Sun public-house at Wapping. Smith and I stole the corpse, and got away with it in a hamper, but as we were driving to St. John's Wood the car we were in came into collision with a lorry. It was very slight and we did not stop, but the hamper, which was on top of the car, fell into the road.

'I began to think that I should never have the opportunity of trying out my experiment in the only possible way to prove that I had mastered the secret of the Black Arts.

'A week passed, and then I had an unexpected stroke of luck. You know what it was, Mr. Quest, so I will only speak of it briefly. Some few years ago I was indirectly concerned in a sensational murder in Paris, and ever since the French Police had been anxious to find me, though they were aware that I could not possibly be convicted on what slender evidence they had.

'Pierre Renault, the detective of the Sûreté, was led to suspect, from a conversation he had overheard between two French crooks, that I was living in London under the name of Burgin. He came across the channel and very stupidly called at my house in Lime Grove to verify his suspicions. It cost him his life.

'That I should allow him to live and cause me trouble was unthinkable, and how better to die than by helping me with my experiment? The chemicals were ready, connected with the bath, and into it went Pierre Renault. In a short time he had ceased to exist. The corrosive fluid had done its work thoroughly. At last, Mr. Quest, I was master of the ancient secret of the Black Arts.'

The doctor paused and mentally reviewed the scene. When he had first seen that he had succeeded his pride knew no bounds.

'With subsequent events you are familiar,' he went on. 'I killed Larry Smith because the police had learned that he had had a hand in the affair at Wapping, and I thought that he might betray me. Not that he knew who I was. I was careful to see to that. But he might have given them some little clue that would have led them to my identity. So it was better that I did not take the risk.

'It was afterwards that you and your friend, Mr. Ferris, had my house kept under surveillance. I was annoyed, and as a challenge to you, and also because I wanted to test the secret again, I got the Scotland Yard watcher into my power. That was a near shave, Mr. Quest, my servant and I had come out to get him when we heard voices and found that he had been joined by Robert Ferris. Fortunately he did not stay very long, and as soon as he had gone we took your man.

'He, too, went into the bath, and that was the complete end of him. There was not a trace of him left when you and Mr. Ferris came with the police, and I was able to snap my fingers at you. It is a truly marvellous thing, that corrosive fluid.'

Quest could contain himself no longer.

'You devil!' he cried, springing to his feet. 'You fiend! If only I had my hands free!'

'Oh, so you are interested, Mr. Quest. I

thought at first that I should bore you.'

Quest bit his lip. Probably the doctor would taunt him with the object of making him lose his nerve, but he would hold on and not give this devil that satisfaction.

'What have you done with David Morley?' he asked quietly, knowing in his heart what the answer would be.

Dr. Burgin shrugged his shoulders.

'Like the others, he has ceased to exist,' he declared.

'So you have murdered him, too. What a monster you are, Burgin.'

Burgin smiled at the detective.

'David Morley was disposed of by my servant, Prantz, half an hour ago. It was to my advantage, from a pecuniary point of view, to remove him from the earth. I don't call it murder, Mr. Quest. It is in the interests of science.'

The detective's horror was too intense for words. He made a futile attempt to snap the cords that bound his wrists, and sank down again in his chair, white to the lips, trembling with fury.

'You fiend!' he gasped. 'No punishment

can possibly fit your crimes.'

'Please let me finish,' the doctor said blandly. 'I was going to tell you that for some time I have been out of chemicals. I sent one of my men, Lubner, to Berlin to purchase a fresh supply, and he arrived by aeroplane soon after you were caught this evening. He and another of my assistants are busy in the laboratory, making a quantity of the corrosive fluid. In a little while I shall dispose of the body of the man you shot this evening, and in case you think that I am boasting of my ability to completely destroy human bodies I should like you to watch the action.'

'That I shall never do!' said Quest fiercely. 'Never!'

'No?' smiled the doctor. 'I think you will, Mr. Quest. In fact you will do exactly as I tell you! And it will be your turn afterwards to go into the bath, my clever detective!'

17

The Race for Help

When Richard Lester left the vicinity of Doomesday House his one thought was to get to Scotland Yard as fast as he possibly could. He had a dim idea of what might have happened to the men who had disappeared, but he was not positive. Quest would never tell him exactly what he had found in the Folio that was housed in the Marazine Library in Paris, but he had gleaned enough to know that however Dr. Burgin had disposed of the bodies it was in an inhuman way.

That Philip Quest should die was bad enough, but that his body, too, would be disposed of was sufficient thought to make him press his foot hard down on the accelerator.

He was some way off the main road, and in trying to take a short cut, as he thought, he went a couple of miles out of his way. The lane he was in was narrow and it would have been impossible to turn the big car, and to back it out would have been a waste of time, and probably land him in the ditch. The only thing to do was to go ahead and watch for the sign posts.

Fifteen minutes later he was on the main road and heading for Romford.

The night was fine, stars shone in a sky of deep blue. The road was empty and he was able to give the car all the speed she could take. At this rate he should be in town in less than the hour.

Robert Ferris, he knew, would be in his office waiting for any message from Quest. Once there he would feel as if the detective stood a chance of being saved. This drive to get aid, taking him away from his partner, seemed to leave him so helpless.

In the distance he could see the reflection of the lights from Romford. There was a red glow in the sky that told him he could not be more than a few miles away. After that Ilford, then through the East End to the City and thence to the Embankment.

The car was behaving splendidly. If he had not been so eager to take a short cut he could have been in Romford now.

Suddenly, out of a side lane, he saw the dim outline of a bicycle. The rider took the corner wide, and in trying to avoid him, for he could not stop the car at the speed he was doing, he swerved and then crashed into a telegraph pole. The grey car turned on its side.

The cyclist had stopped, and when he saw what had happened came pedalling quickly back. Getting off the machine he allowed it to drop onto the grass verge and came over to Lester.

'All right, mate,' he said. 'Hang on a minute, I'll get you out.'

'I'm not hurt,' said Lester. 'This is your fault. Couldn't you see my lights? I might have been killed.'

The cyclist helped him from the car and he stood up.

'Damn silly thing to do!' he snapped. 'You take many more corners like that on the main road and you'll be killed. I tried to avoid knocking you down. The next one might not be so polite.'

'Sorry mate,' said the other. 'But I didn't reckon on you coming up at that speed. You must have been doing seventy.'

'Never mind what I was doing! I'm in a hurry. Help me to get this up.'

They tried to move it, but it was too heavy, and something had happened to the radiator, for water was trickling out on to the road.

'Hell!' growled the young man. 'Now what am I to do? Do you know this place. Can I get a car or taxi near?'

'No, there's nothing near here. Romford is the only place where you'll get a taxi. If you walk hard you'll be in the town in half an hour.'

'Walk! Half an hour!' Lester nearly spat the words at the man. 'Didn't I tell you I was in a hurry. It's a matter of life or death. You can lend me your machine. I'll leave it at a garage and you can collect it.'

'Sorry, mate,' said the man. 'I'm just going on for night duty at the depot. If you're all right I'll be getting on.'

'I'll give you a pound — two pounds!' said Lester. 'Any thing, but for the Lord's sake lend it to me.'

'Can't do it, mate. I've got my job to think of. You'll get a lift, or if you like I'll call in at the garage and tell them to send you a taxi and a breakdown lorry.'

'Oh, go to hell!' said Lester and started to walk in the direction of Romford.

It took him half an hour. In a flat over a chemist shop he saw a light, and knocked hard on the door. The chemist came down and Lester apologised.

'I've had a smash,' he said. 'And it is most important that I get some information through to town. Would you be so kind as to allow me to use your 'phone?'

'Certainly,' said the chemist. 'Come in. Are you hurt?'

'No,' replied Lester. 'The car hit a telegraph pole and turned over.'

The chemist took him through to his office at the back of the shop and directed Lester to the 'phone, which stood on a shelf in the corner.

The call went straight through and in a minute he was talking to Ferris.

He explained to him what had happened to the car, and also what he

236

had heard in the grounds of Doctor Burgin's house.

'I heard the shots,' he continued, 'and then waited for half an hour as Quest had told me. Heaven knows what has happened to him, whether he was killed in the garden or whether that fiend has got him in the house.'

'I'll leave at once,' said Robert Ferris. 'We'll pick you up at Romford police station.'

Lester rang off and went back into the shop where the chemist was waiting.

'Thanks so much,' he said. 'Where is the police station?'

The chemist directed him, and apologising once more for troubling him, Richard Lester made his way to the Romford Police Station, there to wait for the arrival of Robert Ferris.

He gave the desk sergeant particulars of the smash and 'phoned from there to the garage and instructed them to tow the car back and put it right.

18

The Last Moment

For a moment Philip Quest's brain reeled. The cold-blooded way in which the doctor had told him of his end, made him see red, and he turned, cursing the bonds at his wrists that made it impossible for him to take the man by the throat.

'You will kill me, first?' he asked.

Dr. Burgin's eyes twinkled malignantly.

'I hardly think so,' he replied. 'You will see when the time comes.'

As he spoke there was a tap at the door, and Oscar Prantz came in.

'We are ready, sir,' he said.

'Good,' said the doctor. 'Come along, Mr. Quest.'

Taking the detective by the arms the two of them led him from the bedroom and along a corridor to a bathroom, where a powerful light was burning. It was a large room with one window that was shuttered and the tub was a little wider and somewhat longer than the one in the house at Lime Grove.

Stretched at the bottom of it, scantily clad, was the body of the man Lowther — a man of middle age, with sinister features. There was a bullet hole between his eyes.

'This is your victim, Mr. Quest, ready for dissolution,' said Dr. Burgin in a casual voice. 'I went to considerable expense and trouble to equip this place, as well as my residence in St. John's Wood. The arrangements are ingenious, but simple. There are two tanks on the roof, connected with the bath by pipes. Water is forced into the one by hydraulic pressure, and the other — a little smaller — contains the preparation of corrosive chemicals which was employed by those who practised the Black Arts in the olden days. Should I have a visit from the police, however, they would find the small tank empty. They would have their trouble for nothing. They would be utterly baffled.

And now I will show you — '

Pausing, the doctor stepped to the bath and turned on one of the taps. At once there gushed from it, with great force, a thick volume of transparent liquid of a pale brown colour, which filled the room with an acrid smell.

For a few brief moments the body of the man was covered, and Quest, staring in gruesome fascination, such a fascination as a snake exerts over a bird, saw the workings of the diabolical process by which the bodies of Pierre Renault and George Dawe, and David Morley had been destroyed.

Before his eyes the corpse was crumbling, melting, dissolving like wax in a fierce flame, — yielding to the corroding bite of the devilish chemicals, flesh and hair, bones and clothing.

Gradually, yet swiftly, it faded from sight, and meanwhile, the fluid, which had been shut off at the tap, turned to the dark, cloudy colour of a swampy pool. Soon also, only a bare and grinning skull was visible, and that, too, quickly disappeared.

In ten minutes it was all over.

Dr. Burgin lifted the plug now, and turned on the other tap, and a rushing volume of water rapidly emptied the tub of the horrid blend of chemicals and humanity.

'You — you fiend!' gasped Quest.

Dr. Burgin laughed.

'Murder made easy,' he remarked. 'An invention that is worth fortunes to a man without scruples. The secrets of the Black Arts applied to modern crime. A secret that has been buried for centuries in the old manuscript, and unearthed by myself.

'You have a knowledge of analytical science, Mr. Quest,' he added, 'and I would give you a full account of my discovery, if I had the time to spare. But I have not. In half an hour it will be your turn.'

Quest did not reply. They took him back to the bedroom and he was left there alone, sick at heart, to wait for the end. Very soon he, too, would cease to exist. He felt that nothing could avert his fate. It would be foolish to hope.

* * *

Something must have gone wrong and caused delay for nearly an hour had passed before Dr. Burgin appeared. Oscar Prantz was not with him. He was accompanied by two rough looking men one of whom was doubtless the man Lubner.

'The time has come, Mr. Quest,' the doctor said quietly.

Philip Quest made no protest, no appeal, though the very thought of the horror that awaited him was enough to have driven him mad.

He was now almost certain that the worst was in store for him, for he noticed that the doctor's companions wore gloves — rubber gloves.

But in silence, resolved not to show the least sign of fear, he let the two men conduct him to the bathroom, where he saw at a glance that the tub had already been half filled with the brown liquid.

Dr. Burgin looked rather grave, and observing this, Quest judged that he was somewhat apprehensive because of the delay, and that Oscar Prantz was keeping watch in the garden. And this was exactly the cause of the doctor's expression. In preparing the fluid for the destruction of the detective the doctor's assistant had made a mistake in the amounts, and this meant that a second tankful had to be prepared. Time was important for the doctor, for if the detective's partner had accompanied Quest here, then he would have gone for help, and in that event a rescue party might arrive at any moment.

Quest, however, had put the thought of being saved from this madman out of his head. He was sure that Lester and Ferris could not possibly arrive in time.

'Lubner, bind his ankles,' said the doctor. 'Be quick about it. I don't want to waste any more time.'

The command could only mean one thing. It was to be the worst possible death. He was not even to be drugged. He was to be put into the bath alive — and conscious!

While his ankles were being tied he turned suddenly faint and dizzy, and reeled to the wall, a mist swimming before his eyes, and of what happened at that moment he retained no clear recollection afterwards.

Vaguely, indistinctly, he heard shouts and curses, and, as one sees in a dream, he saw a blur of moving, scuffling figures.

It was not until he came to his full senses and gazed about him with an unclouded mind, that he realised that he had been rescued at the last minute.

The room was full of men. He recognised Robert Ferris and Lester, and several men from the Yard. Dr. Burgin stood at one side, his arms folded, and a vicious glitter in his eyes, a look of defiance on his face. Man of iron that he was, only a slight pallor marked the chaos of his inner thoughts.

The man Lubner lay huddled on the floor, and standing by him were Oscar Prantz and the doctor's assistant, the latter with his wrists in handcuffs.

The police were guarding all the prisoners.

Quest suddenly realised that Lester was shaking him, speechless with emotion, and Robert Ferris was talking to him.

'Quest! Quest! Wake up. It's all right, we're here. We got here in time.'

Philip Quest looked at them in silence for a moment.

'He seems to be half-dazed,' said Lester.

'Hello!' said the detective. 'I'm so glad you got here in time. Did I pass out? Sorry. It was terrible!'

Quest shuddered at the recollection.

'What were they going to do with you?' asked Ferris. 'What is that stuff in the bath?'

'A powerful corrosive fluid,' said Quest. 'A diabolical invention of that fiend's. I was to have been dropped into it — put in alive.'

'And what would have happened?'

'In a few minutes I should have been eaten away, Ferris. There would have been nothing left of me, body or clothes.'

'Nothing left of you? It's incredible.'

'It's true!' declared the detective. 'The suspicions I had about the doctor's secret were quite right. You will be shocked when I tell you everything.'

He turned to Lester.

'I owe my life to you,' he said. 'You must have been very quick. I didn't think you could possibly arrive so soon.'

'I didn't get to town,' said Lester. 'I had a smash near Romford, and had to walk to there. I thought it would be better to phone Mr. Ferris than waste time hiring cars or going by train. I waited at Romford for the Yard cars and they picked me up there. We drove as fast as we could, stopped three or four hundred yards from the house, and walked the rest of the way. I don't think the car is very badly damaged.'

Quest smiled weakly.

'Don't let that worry you,' he said.

'Have you seen anything of David Morley?' asked Lester. 'You believed he was here. Did you find him?'

'He was here,' said Quest bitterly. 'But you were too late to save him. He was murdered earlier in the evening.'

'In — in the bath?'

'Yes — in the bath,' said Quest, and looking at Dr. Burgin Lester saw him give a defiant smile.

'Poor fellow!' exclaimed Robert Ferris.

'What a tragedy! It might have been prevented, Quest, if we had all come together tonight. It is a great pity we didn't.'

'If you remember,' said Quest, 'you were not willing to take action until you were sure my suspicions were right.'

'That's true. It was my mistake. There's no use talking of it now.'

'How did you manage to get in here?' asked the detective.

'When we arrived outside the drive the house appeared to be in darkness. There were twelve of us and so we walked straight up the gravel path. We had gone more than half way when we came upon Oscar Prantz. He was keeping watch, and instead of giving the alarm he brought us into the house and led us upstairs.'

'The servant did that?' asked Quest. 'I am surprised.'

'I suppose the sight of so many of us put the wind up him. I expect he thought that by helping us he would save his own neck. He knew the game was up.'

Dr. Burgin had been apparently absorbed in thought. He appeared to have paid no

247

heed to the conversation, but really he had heard every word. Now his expression altered, and the palor of his face changed to a deep red.

'It's a lie! Prantz would not do such a thing!'

'Ask him,' said Ferris curtly.

There was no need for the doctor to ask. One look at his servant's face told him all he wanted to know.

'So you have betrayed me, Prantz,' he said in a dull, quiet voice, as if he was more hurt than angry.

'If you want to call it that, sir,' Oscar Prantz replied.

'You, the man who has been so loyal and devoted to me for years. I trusted you. Why did you do it?'

'I thought it would be to my interests, sir. The police had arrived, and there were too many for us to handle. Furthermore I wished to prevent you murdering Mr. Quest.'

'Indeed! So that was the reason? Well, I won't say anything more, except that you will be disappointed if you hope to be dealt with leniently because you have — '

As Dr. Burgin spoke he sprang suddenly at his servant, and with an oath he seized him by the throat.

'You cur!' he snarled. 'You treacherous cur!'

Oscar Prantz was stronger than he looked. At once he wrenched himself free, and as quickly he struck with his clenched fist. The blow, landing on the doctor's chin, sent him staggering.

He reeled against the bath, and the next instant, before anybody could grasp him, he pitched backward over the low rim of it, screaming as he fell.

Two of the men who had come with Ferris from Scotland Yard went quickly to the bath, their intention being to get the doctor out.

'Don't touch him!' cried Quest loudly. 'You can't save him! Don't go near. It would be certain death!'

It was a dreadful sight, the end of Dr. Burgin. Standing aloof, dumb with horror, Robert Ferris, Lester, and the Scotland Yard men, saw what Quest had seen before — the ghastly process of dissolution. They gazed spellbound, as if they could not believe their eyes.

Again and again the doctor struggled to rise, splashing and floundering, clawing in vain at the slippery edges of the bath, while shrieks of maddening, agonising torture poured incessantly from his lips.

At length his shrieks were stifled, and he was unrecognisable, bearing scarcely any resemblance to human form, when what was left sank down for the last time, his clothing and skin eaten off.

He was entirely submerged now in the corrosive fluid, and lay quite still. His body rapidly dissolved, crumbling to putrefaction, and from putrefaction to shadowy fragments which were scarcely visible.

They, too, soon melted into the thick, brown liquid, and when the chemicals had thoroughly done their work, Quest lifted the vent plug and turned on the water tap.

19

A Surprise for Philip Quest

As soon as Philip Quest sent the remains of Dr. Burgin out of the bath he suggested that they should all retire to a more pleasant room.

All who had witnessed the horrible spectacle were badly shaken, and felt very sick. Some of the Scotland Yard men looked a little green. Hard-bitten and used to tragedy as they were, this had shocked them beyond words. It had made as deep an impression on Oscar Prantz as on the rest. He was trembling like a leaf, as was the handcuffed man.

Lubner, the German, had seen nothing. He had been stunned by a blow when he offered resistance to the police on their entry into the room. He lay prostrate on the floor.

When they went into the library Quest walked over to a side table which held a liberal supply of spirits. He poured out three stiff whiskies and took them over to where Ferris and Lester had seated themselves. He told the men to have a drink.

'I expect you can do with it,' he said, and the men signified, by a rapid approach to the table, their gratitude.

Robert Ferris was badly upset. With an unsteady hand he mopped the beads of perspiration from his brow.

'It was awful! Awful!' he declared. 'I shouldn't have believed it. So that is how Pierre Renault died in the house in Lime Grove.'

'Yes,' said the detective. 'Pierre Renault and George Dawe. David Morley was disposed of in this house tonight, as was the body of the man I killed in the garden when we had the fight.'

'And you would have had the same end, Quest?' asked Ferris.

'Most certainly, had you not arrived in time. I was to have gone in the bath alive. That was the doctor's fiendish intention. They were binding my ankles when — '

There was an interruption from Oscar

Prantz, who, with the other two men had been brought into the library.

'Did you say Mr. Morley was dead, sir?' he asked.

'Yes,' said Quest.

'You are wrong, sir,' said the servant. 'Mr. Morley is not dead.'

Quest stared incredulously.

'Not dead!' he exclaimed. 'But the doctor told me — '

'Dr. Burgin told you a lie, sir. Or, to be correct, he told you what he believed to be true.'

'What are you saying? Is this true?'

'Yes, sir. Mr. Morley is alive.'

'And in this house?'

'In this house, Mr. Quest. You see Dr. Burgin had the gift of magnetic powers. He had me completely under a spell as it were, from the time I entered his service. I was compelled to do his bidding. I had no will-power of my own. I can say I was hypnotised by — '

'Nonsense!' Quest broke in. 'Don't expect me to believe such rubbish.'

'It is not rubbish, sir,' protested the man. 'If you will allow me to explain more clearly — '

'Never mind that. What about David Morley?'

'I will tell you in a few words, sir. The young gentleman was unconscious, he had been drugged. I was told by the doctor to dispose of him in the bath, and later, when he enquired of me, I said that I had done so. But I had not. I put Mr. Morley into a large cupboard in his bedroom, and he is there now.'

'You did that because you feared a police raid here tonight?' asked Quest.

'It was partly for that reason I will admit,' replied Prantz. 'After you were caught in the garden I had an idea that there had been somebody with you, and that it would not be long before the police arrived. At the same time, though, I was sorry for the young man. I had taken a liking to him, and in any case I should have tried to save him.'

'Well, now you can show us where he is.'

'Yes, sir, if you will accompany me — '

At that instant the door was pushed open and David Morley tottered unsteadily into the room. He was very pale and lurched as he walked. He threw a sweeping glance around him, and then his eyes rested on Philip Quest.

'Thank heaven!' he cried. 'I was sure you were here.'

Quest had risen as the young man came into the room, and now he eased him into the chair.

'Sit down, Morley.' And then to Lester. 'Get him a stiff brandy, there is some on the table.'

In a few seconds Richard Lester came back with the drink, which David Morley gulped gratefully.

'I think I have been drugged, Mr. Quest,' he said. 'A little while ago I came to my senses and found myself in a cupboard, in my room. I was trying to get out of the house when I heard people talking in the bathroom. I crept to the door and listened. I recognised your voice and — '

He broke off and a look of terror came into his eyes.

'What happened?' he asked. 'The doctor told me about the bath. He said I was going in it.' He looked round the room at the men. 'Who are these men?' he asked of Quest. 'And where is the doctor? Have you arrested him?'

'No,' said the detective gravely. 'The doctor has ceased to exist. He is dead, killed by his own terrible invention.'

'In the bath?'

'Yes, he fell in.'

In a few words Quest related the events of that evening and gave a brief description of Dr. Burgin's end, sparing the young man the hideous details, for he could see that Morley had had enough to frighten him, without fraying his nerves with a recital of what had occurred.

'Frightful and agonising though it was,' he continued, 'it was a lesser punishment than the scoundrel deserved. It is impossible to feel any pity for him.'

'When he was talking to you did he tell you what grudge he had against me?' asked Morley. 'Did he explain the mystery?'

'He merely remarked that it would be to his advantage if you were dead. That was all. Didn't he give you an explanation?'

'No, he refused to speak of it, though I questioned him several times since I was kidnapped and brought here. I am no wiser than I was, Mr. Quest.'

Quest turned to the servant.

'You were in Dr. Burgin's confidence, Prantz,' he said. 'What was the reason for the numerous attacks on Mr. Morley, and the kidnapping?'

'I don't know, sir,' said the servant.

'You must know,' said the detective. 'We heard the doctor say he had trusted you. He must have told you.'

'It is as much a mystery to me as to you, sir. It has been from the first.'

'I don't believe you!' snapped the detective. 'You assisted the doctor in his crimes.'

'I did,' said Prantz, 'but against my will. The doctor was a peculiar man, and for some reason he kept me in ignorance in regard to Mr. Morley. I have never questioned him. He would not have allowed that.'

'You are sure you have no idea why the

young man was kidnapped?'

'I have not, Mr. Quest. If I had I would readily tell you. I should have nothing to gain by refusing.'

This last statement was true, and it convinced Quest that the servant, who had saved the life of the doctor's intended victim and had helped the police, was not trying to deceive him.

'You were at least aware that a man by the name of Juan Ramenez was concerned in this mystery?' said Quest.

'No, sir, I was not,' answered Prantz in surprise.

'You knew that he was a friend of the doctor's?'

'I have heard Dr. Burgin speak of him.'

'In what connection?'

'He mentioned the gentleman as a friend he had known abroad and was now living in London.'

'Have you ever seen Ramenez?'

'No, sir. Never. He has never been to the house in Lime Grove.'

'Has he been to Doomesday House since you came here with Dr. Burgin?'

'No, sir.'

Philip Quest believed these statements. The man was ready to talk if there was anything to be told, he knew that.

He had learned, during the time he had had Dr. Burgin and Ramenez watched that, with the exception of the two visits to Doomesday House, they had met only at luncheons in West End restaurants. Probably the Spaniard had stipulated that the motives for the designs on David Morley were on no account to be disclosed to Oscar Prantz, and the doctor had agreed to this.

The injured man had by now recovered. He gave the name of Crawley, and both he and Lubner, questioned by the detective, declared they had no more knowledge of the matter than Oscar Prantz.

David Morley was bewildered. He had been sure that at least the doctor's servant would be able to give the information he so badly wanted.

'If you ask me,' said Robert Ferris, 'the mystery will never be cleared up.'

Quest shrugged his shoulders.

'It will be,' he replied. 'I shall find a way

to open Juan Ramenez's lips.'

'He knows there is not a shred of evidence against him,' said Ferris, 'and he will defy you. He will refuse to speak. He has covered his tracks well. There is nothing you can do to bring him into this.'

'He won't get the better of me,' said the detective. 'Soon after he came into the case I formed a theory, one which I have kept to myself. The only one which can possibly account for — '

He broke off and looked at his watch.

'It is well past midnight, and time we were going. We'll leave a couple of the men in charge here, Ferris, and as soon as we get to town you send a couple more to take possession of the house in Lime Grove. Tomorrow we will make a search there and destroy certain things, including that pernicious treatise on the Black Arts, and the formula for the composition of chemicals. I dare say we shall find it in the house.'

'Morley, you can go back to Beverly Street now. There is nothing more to be afraid of. By the way, the story of this awful affair must not get into the papers, before tomorrow night at the least. This applies to everybody,' he said, looking round the room at the men Ferris had brought with him. 'Say nothing about it. If Juan Ramenez should hear of the raid tonight he will take to his heels, and probably get out of the country.'

A few minutes later the house of horror was deserted, except for the two Scotland Yard men who were to remain on duty, and the rest of the party were on their way back to London with their prisoners.

20

Juan Ramenez Explains

It was broad daylight before Philip Quest got to bed the next morning. It was his intention to return to Doomesday House in the course of the day, but unforeseen events were to compel him to postpone that trip.

The happenings of the previous night had rather shaken him, and it was a long time before he could get to sleep. Had he been left alone he would probably have slept through the whole of the day, but the entrance of Lester wakened him.

'I've been up for over an hour,' he said.

'Have you been out?' asked the detective, as his eye caught the paper which the young man held in his hand.

'Yes, I went for a walk. Sorry to disturb you, but I thought you ought to see this.'

He handed Quest an early copy of the

evening paper, and pointed to a paragraph that ran as follows:

'It is rumoured that a party of Scotland Yard men, accompanied by Mr. Philip Quest, raided a country house in Essex last night, belonging to Dr. Francis Burgin of St. John's Wood, and that sensational disclosures may be expected.'

Quest frowned.

'It is just what I wished to prevent,' he declared. 'One of Ferris' men must have talked. It is not the first time this sort of thing has happened. It may do great harm.'

'You think Juan Ramenez will clear out if he has read this paragraph?' asked Lester.

'He might, and he might not. Probably he would, no matter how secure he might feel. What time is it?'

'Five o'clock in the afternoon.'

'And that paper is out at three. That is two hours wasted. You had better go along to St. James's and keep an eye on the building where Ramenez lives.'

'And then what?'

'If he leaves, you follow him to

wherever he goes, and then report to me. If I don't hear from you I will join you there in a couple of hours. I must have a talk with Ferris first.'

'Right you are, Mr. Quest.'

Lester was gone in a quarter of an hour, and by then the detective was up and in his bath. As soon as he had had something to eat he made his way to Scotland Yard, where he discussed with Robert Ferris the question of issuing a warrant for the arrest of Juan Ramenez.

Ferris was of the opinion that it would be impossible to get any evidence which would implicate the Spaniard in the abduction of David Morley, and Quest reluctantly agreed with him. He was pretty sure, however, that he would be able to force a confession from the man.

They drove from Scotland Yard to Beverly Street, and had a talk with David Morley.

The knowledge that he need no longer fear kidnapping or death had made a great difference to that young man. He looked much better, more like the man Philip Quest had once admired as a specimen of good health and sensibility.

Very little was said about the events at Doomesday House.

'Lester is watching the building where Ramenez lives,' said Quest, after they had been talking for a few minutes, 'and he will follow him if he goes out. I'm going to see Ramenez, and I want you to come with me.'

'What can I do?' asked Morley.

'If my suspicions are correct I shall need you,' said the detective. 'I'm not quite certain if my surmise is correct, but we can soon find that out.'

'If there is anything I can do to help clear up the mystery concerning the attempts on my life,' said the young man, 'you know I will. I'll get my clothes and come with you.'

The three of them went back to the detective's offices and found that Lester had returned.

'Your bird has flown,' were his first words.

'Gone?' Quest exclaimed. 'What a pity! How did you find that out? Did you see the hall porter?'

'No, I didn't,' said his partner. 'I watched the building for half an hour, and then Juan Ramenez came out, carrying a suitcase. He walked down to Piccadilly and picked up a taxi. I took another and followed him to Waterloo. I shadowed him closely to the main line booking office and heard him ask for a first-class single to Southampton. The train he went by left at twenty minutes past six.'

Quest's gloomy face brightened a little.

'So Ramenez has gone to Southampton,' he said. 'I wonder what his plans are. He can't cross to the Channel Islands or to St. Malo tonight, if that was his intention, for the last boat sails at seven-thirty. Perhaps — '

He went over to his desk and picked up a newspaper. Opening it he searched among the pages until he came to the sailing list.

'No liner sails for New York tonight or tomorrow,' he stated, 'and no Royal Mail Steamer for South America for two days. I dare say we shall find him at Southampton, Lester.'

He turned to the Scotland Yard man.

'Can I have one of your cars, Ferris? Mine is in the wilds of Essex and the Lord knows when it will be ready.'

'Certainly,' said Ferris. 'I'll phone for one now. It can be here in fifteen minutes.'

He did this, and they waited impatiently until a blast from the horn of a car told them that the vehicle was outside.

Ferris did not go with them. He had work to do, and knew that Quest, Lester and young Morley would be able to do all that was necessary.

A few minutes later they were speeding across London in the powerful police car.

The suburbs left behind they covered the miles very rapidly, and ran into Southampton shortly after ten o'clock. The car was left at the local police station, and the three men then began their search of the hotels.

At the large hotels their enquiries proved fruitless, and it was at a modest one that they eventually got the information they wanted.

'Yes, sir,' said the manager, 'there is a

gentleman answering that description here. He arrived about nine o'clock. I should have taken him to be a Spaniard, but he gave the name of Fowler.'

'Is he in now?' asked Quest.

'Yes, he had dinner and went to his room afterwards.'

'Well, we wish to see him. There is no need to announce us. We will go up at once.'

The manager summoned a page-boy, and the lad conducted them to a room on the first floor. The door was not locked. Quest opened it and stepped quickly inside with his companions. The hand in his pocket grasped a pistol, but that was not necessary.

Juan Ramenez was standing by the window, smoking a cigar. He turned round, and for an instant he showed both fear and consternation. Then he shrugged his shoulders and a look of defiance crept into his eyes.

'Hullo, Morley!' he said amiably. 'You here. Will you introduce me to your friends?'

David Morley was flushed with anger.

'This is Mr. Philip Quest, the private detective,' he replied coldly, 'and the other gentleman is his partner, Richard Lester.'

Quest smiled.

'I think the formality of an introduction could have been dispensed with, Mr. Ramenez,' he said. 'You knew who we were.'

'I did not,' Ramenez answered. 'I have never seen either of you before.'

'Possibly not. Maybe I was wrong there, but anyway, you know of us.'

Ramenez did not answer.

'And what brought you here, Mr. Ramenez?' asked the detective. 'Did the paragraph in the paper frighten you?'

'Paragraph in the paper? What are you talking about? I don't understand you.'

'I mean the notice in the paper relating to the police raid on Dr. Burgin's house in Essex.'

'Oh, no. Nothing of the sort.'

'Then why did you hurry off to Southampton?'

'For a very simple reason, Mr. Quest. I was going to pay a short visit to St. Malo, in Brittany. I haven't been feeling too well and I thought the sea air would do me good. I am sailing tomorrow. As for the newspaper paragraph you referred to, I did not see it.'

Quest smiled. There was no need to hurry. They had Ramenez here, and that was the most important thing. He could talk for an hour, but eventually the Spaniard would give him the information he was determined to get. The reason for the attacks on Morley.

'You are a friend of Dr. Burgin's, I believe?'

'He is not a friend of mine. He is a mere acquaintance, and a man I have always mistrusted. It would not surprise me to hear that he was in the hands of the police.'

Juan Ramenez was perfectly self-possessed, quite at his ease.

Though he could not have any knowledge of Dr. Burgin's death, the paragraph in the paper had led him to believe that the doctor had been arrested, and therefore he was afraid of being denounced.

Quest realised that he must be cautious.

'I know a great deal about Dr. Burgin myself,' he continued. 'I have been trying for a long while to get evidence against him, and to account for his designs on David Morley. After several futile attempts he succeeded in having this young man abducted, and it was his intention to murder him.'

'He would not have murdered my friend Morley!' exclaimed Ramenez.

'Yes, he would. And you were a party to the conspiracy,' said Quest.

Ramenez smiled.

'My dear Mr. Quest, this is ridiculous!' he said. 'How could the death of my friend be to my advantage?'

'I will tell you in a few words,' said the detective. 'Because he is your nephew!'

It was a chance shot. Quest had not been positive his guess was right. But he had launched the bolt, and it had shot home.

Juan Ramenez's pale twitching features betrayed him. He bit his lip, and averted his eyes from David Morley, who stared at him in bewilderment.

'My uncle?' he gasped. 'My father's brother? Is this true, Ramenez?'

Juan Ramenez shook his head.

'No, Mr. Quest has made a mistake,' he asserted doggedly.

David Morley turned to the detective.

'I can't trace any likeness,' he declared.

'Do you remember your uncle?' asked Quest.

'I have a clear recollection of him, though he disappeared when I was quite young.'

'Did he bear any mark by which he could be identified, Morley?'

'Yes, when he and my father were boys each tattooed the family crest on the chest of the other. I remember my father telling me about it.'

Philip Quest smiled grimly.

'Then perhaps you will show us your chest, Ramenez.'

Juan Ramenez let his hands drop to his side.

'I am Peter Morley,' he admitted, and there was a note of sorrow and shame in his voice. 'There is no use denying it.'

There was a brief silence. The revelation was a complete surprise to Lester, and to David Morley it was a numbing shock.

'You had better know that Burgin is dead,' said Quest to the wretched man. 'His fate was more than he deserved. He fell by accident into a bath of that terrible fluid he invented.

'You are a scoundrel,' he continued. 'It is not for me to judge you too harshly, but I fear that, apart from the conspiracy you entered into with Dr. Burgin you knew of the murders he committed. You know what happened to the French detective and to the Scotland Yard man, Dawe.'

'You are wrong,' Peter Morley replied in a dull voice. 'Though I had my suspicions I knew nothing of the persons referred to except what I read in the papers. Did Dr. Burgin confess before he died? Did he implicate me?'

'No, he did not. But I had the story of his past life from his own lips.'

'Then I had better tell you everything,' said the man, 'I was much younger than my brother, Geoffrey, and I was the black

273

sheep of the family. I got into trouble in England and had to leave the country. I drifted to the Continent, and spent a number of years there, living by my wits and under various names. I first met Dr. Burgin in Vienna, and became very intimate with him. We went to Munich together, and it was at that time the false report of my death appeared in the English and European papers. I had been robbed of papers which disclosed my real identity. The man who stole them was drowned, and the papers were found on him.

'After I parted company with Dr. Burgin I was in an Austrian prison for several years. I was released and then made my way to Spain. There my wits and my education were practically my only assets, and when I had accumulated sufficient money I came back to England, and posed as a Spaniard. I took a flat in St. James' and with my money was able to make an entry into a certain section of society.

'It was at a reception in the West End that I fell in with Dr. Burgin again, and the next day I accompanied him to his place in Essex. There he told me of his horrible discovery — the corrosive fluid that would quickly dispose of a human body.

'He was acquainted with my family affairs, and knowing that in the event of my nephew's death I could claim the estate, he proposed to put David Morley out of existence in consideration of a large sum of money. I refused to listen to it at first, but the temptation was strong. The boy was young, and might outlive me. Further he might marry, and then I should lose the estate. In the end the doctor won me over. I consented to his proposition.

'It was arranged that after the death of David I should disappear for a time, cut off my beard and moustache, and turn up in my real name to claim his possessions. I should not have incurred any risk in doing so, for there was nothing against me in England, except heavy debts.

'Though you may not believe me, Mr. Quest, I have suffered from remorse ever since I yielded to the temptation. I would have backed out if I could, but I dare not. Dr. Burgin would not hear of it. He knew I was wanted by the police in Switzerland, and he threatened to have me extradited to that country.

'When I read that paragraph in the paper I thought that the doctor had been arrested, and knowing the character of the man felt certain that he would give me away. My only hope was to get out of the country. I came hurriedly down to Southampton, and if you had not caught me I would have sailed for New York in a day or so.'

Peter Morley paused.

'How did you find out I was here, Mr. Quest?' he asked. 'Nobody knew of my plans.'

'My partner was watching your residence,' said the detective. 'He saw you come out and followed you to Waterloo. At the booking office he heard you ask for the ticket to Southampton.'

'What are you going to do with me?' he asked the detective.

In the silence that followed David Morley looked appealingly at Quest.

'Let me decide, Mr. Quest,' he urged. 'My uncle does not deserve any mercy, I know. But Dr. Burgin is dead, and I am quite safe now. Actually he had nothing to do with the crimes. For my sake, please let him go.'

Philip Quest hesitated, his face cold and stern.

'You ought to spend the rest of your life in prison,' he said. 'For your nephew's sake I will take no action — on condition that you leave this country within twenty-four hours. Should you ever return I shall have no hesitation in exposing you.'

The man's face was a mixture of gratitude and amazement.

'You — you mean — I — Oh, thank you!'

'Don't thank me!' snapped Quest. 'I'm doing this because of your nephew. He has a decent reputation and I'd like to spare him the humiliation of having a man like you known as a relative.'

'I don't deserve — '

His voice choked, and he stood in silence, with bowed head, as Quest and his companions passed out of the room.

No crime in living memory, if, indeed, any in the past, roused such wide-spread horror as did the infamies of Dr. Francis Burgin. No immediate steps were taken in regard to his two residences. They were left in the care of the police, with doors locked and sealed, until the trial of Oscar Prantz and the men Lubner and Crawley, which was not long delayed.

Counsel for the Crown — previously instructed by Philip Quest — wove a net round Oscar Prantz, and he was convicted and sentenced to death. The other men each received five years imprisonment, their defence being that they had had no hand in the actual crimes. Subsequently Oscar Prantz was reprieved in consideration of what he had done on the night of the police raid.

On the week following the trial David Morley and Carol Renoff were married, and on the following day Quest and Robert Ferris motored down to Doomesday House and destroyed all the chemicals in the doctor's laboratory. When this had been done they returned to town, went to the house in Lime Grove, and destroyed the chemicals there also.

The ancient manuscript, dealing with the Black Arts was still in the cabinet, and much to his satisfaction Quest found in a desk the formula for the corrosive fluid. Both were placed in the grate, a match applied, and the two men watched the papers consumed to ashes.

'I wish I could do the same with the manuscript in the Magazine Library,' said the detective.

'It will be quite safe there,' said Ferris. 'I don't suppose the secret will ever be discovered by a second Dr. Burgin.'

THE END

We do hope that you have enjoyed reading this large print book.

Did you know that all of our titles are available for purchase?

We publish a wide range of high quality large print books including:
Romances, Mysteries, Classics
General Fiction
Non Fiction and Westerns

Special interest titles available in large print are:
The Little Oxford Dictionary
Music Book, Song Book
Hymn Book, Service Book

Also available from us courtesy of Oxford University Press:
Young Readers' Dictionary
(large print edition)
Young Readers' Thesaurus
(large print edition)

For further information or a free brochure, please contact us at:
Ulverscroft Large Print Books Ltd.,
The Green, Bradgate Road, Anstey,
Leicester, LE7 7FU, England.
Tel: (00 44) 0116 236 4325
Fax: (00 44) 0116 234 0205

Other titles in the
Linford Mystery Library:

FOUR CORPSES IN A MILLION

John Robb

This is the story of a master criminal and his scheme to rule England. The one thing he must have is money. Four people have to die in order that his plan might not be frustrated. This is also the story of Roger Ferningham, who cheated death three times — and of Anne, who loved him. It is also the story of Biggs, the Cockney, without whom Roger could not have won through . . .

THE PHANTOM SLAYER

Derwent Steele

In London, criminals are being murdered — following lucrative crimes such as the jewel heist pulled off by Lew Steen. Like all the others, Steen receives a letter requesting a meeting — which must be attended — where the sender will buy the loot. However, the rock-bottom price on offer cannot be refused: those that refuse, die — horribly, from poison gas! Little wonder that the popular press labels their assailant as *The Phantom Slayer*. He has to be stopped — but how?